SAFER THAN LOVE

N LOVE

Margery Allingham

Chive   ll & Co.
Bath, England   ˜   Thorndike, Maine USA

This Large Print edition is published by Chivers Press, England, and by G.K. Hall & Co., USA.

Published in 2000 in the U.K. by arrangement with Sexton Agency & Press Ltd.

Published in 2000 in the U.S. by arrangement with John Stevens Robling, Ltd.

U.K. Hardcover   ISBN 0-7540-4206-5   (Chivers Large Print)
U.K. Softcover   ISBN 0-7540-4207-3   (Camden Large Print)
U.S. Softcover   ISBN 0-7838-9096-6   (Nightingale Series Edition)

The text of this Large Print edition is unabridged.
Other aspects of the book may vary from the original edition.

Set in 16 pt. New Times Roman.

Printed in Great Britain on acid-free paper.

British Library Cataloguing in Publication Data available

Library of Congress Cataloging-in-Publication Data

Allingham, Margery, 1904–1966.
    Safer than love / Margery Allingham.
        p. cm.
    ISBN 0-7838-9096-6 (lg. print : sc : alk. paper)
    1. Widows—Fiction. 2. Large type books. I. Title.
PR6001.L678 S24 2000
823'.912—dc21   00–031899

PART ONE

I suppose the most frightening thing in the world is the moment when one realises that courage isn't going to be enough. One plods along cheerfully, convinced that one hasn't got a breaking point, and then, quite suddenly and at the most unlikely moment, one sees it, not yet quite on top of one but not so far ahead.

That was why I crossed the road before old Mrs. Wycherley caught sight of me. I had nothing against her, poor old darling. She was kindness personified, and the canon's sister, but I knew that in less than five minutes I should be seeing her sad eyes peering out of her unpowdered face, should be feeling her gloved hand on my arm, and, out of a warm cloud of cologne and mouthwash, should hear her soft voice saying: "How *are* we today, my dear? Forgive me, but you look so *young*." And I felt I couldn't stand it.

Mrs. Wycherley always said that. At first I had assumed that she was worrying because I didn't start a baby, but just lately it had dawned upon me that she was only guessing, with the rest of the insatiably inquisitive town of Tinworth, and was enquiring if I *could* be happily married. So far I had always been brightly reassuring but this morning, the moment I saw her black drapery bearing down upon me, I turned and fled across the glistening surface of Tortham Road, panic-stricken. It alarmed me all the more because I had not dreamed that I could ever be the sort of person. Until then I should have said that I was a young woman who didn't hold with panic. I hurried down the Tortham Road, giddy with the shock of the discovery.

Every provincial town of any size in southern England has its own Tortham Road under some name or other. It is the good road, the residential street leading off the main shopping centre where, in their heyday some eighty years ago, Victorian merchants built their little mansions. These still squat there, portly and inconvenient, each boldly individual in style to the point of mock-Gothic turrets or pagoda-topped conservatories, and each muffled like a sleeping beauty in thickets of laurel and rhododendron. Now, of course, they are nearly all nursing homes, or converted flats, or schools. Our school, the one of which my husband was Headmaster was at the far end of Tortham Road, and our estate marked the end of the town and the beginning of the fields. The main house, dominating the four others put up to form dormitories for the boys, really was a mansion. It had been modernised, but the broad Georgian façade, glowing in rose brick at the far end of wide lawns, had been built by a retiring Tinworth banker at the time of the great merger, and it still bore his name.

Buchanan House was a first-class private preparatory school and little boys came there

4

as boarders from all over the country to be made ready for Tortham College, which could hold its own with—well, if not quite with Eton, at least with most of the others.

Tinworth was delighted with Buchanan House. As a market town with a side line in the manufacture of agricultural implements, it did not set out to be particularly intellectual itself, but it liked its school and liked it all the more because there was nothing state-aided about it. Parents paid and paid highly, and their money went out into the town's trade. Ratepayers, startled by the demands of the County Council for the new education account, felt that was as it should be.

As headmasters go, Victor was young. He was in his late thirties and was thought to be brilliant. Indeed, if all I'd been told was true, Tinworth was prepared to credit him with the brain of an Einstein and the knowledge of an encyclopedia, but that did not prevent it from speculating with uncanny insight about his private life. I was beginning to realise that after my six months of marriage to him.

I was walking very fast, almost running, the shopping basket I carried for show swinging on my arm and my straw hat flapping. I was forgetting my dignity and trying to forget everything else, including the atmosphere I had come out to escape, not to mention my latest irritation, which was the news that Andy Durtham, of all people, was going to take a locum job here in Tinworth for Dr. Browning while the old man went on holiday.

Dorothy's letter mentioning this somewhat startling news amid a host of other gossip from St. Jude's, where she was still a Sister, was in my pocket. It had only arrived that morning but as usual there was no telling when she had written it. Dorothy wrote letters as some people knit woollies, now and again when the mood took her. It was sometimes possible, by carefully noting the changes of ink in the closely scribbled pages, to discover if any particular item was some months old or comparatively recent, and I was just wondering if I could pull the untidy bundle out and examine it again there and then in the street when I saw Maureen Jackson thumping down the sidewalk towards me.

Miss Jackson was the Headmaster's secretary and, I suppose, about five years older than I was. The notion that the Head's wife was always older than the Head's secretary had made our relationship, I thought, vaguely awkward at first, but she appeared to have decided to 'settle all that' in her cheerfully efficient way by treating me always with bluff kindliness, as if I was not quite right in the head or a foreigner. So far I had not attempted to enlighten her, because she was Tinworth personified and I was trying very hard to get the hang of Tinworth.

Miss Jackson was the daughter of the town's

best auctioneer and estate agent, quite a powerful person in that community, and her relatives seemed to spread into every conceivable branch of the town's affairs. Her grandfather had been Mayor seven times. Her uncle was the owner of the great ironmongers and agricultural engineers in the High Street. Her mother was an Urban District Councillor, and at least two of her brothers were Justices of the Peace.

She came thumping towards me, big, bony, and not uncomely, with a pink and white face and clear cold blue eyes which were somehow typical of Tinworth in their bland, self-satisfied intelligence. She was known as the 'thundering English rose' by the junior masters, whom she used to treat with offhand tolerance. I understood her work was excellent and she certainly took Victor's acid rebukes with amiable forbearance.

'Morning!' she shouted at me when we were within hailing distance. 'The vac is heaven, isn't it? Or don't you like it?'

Her last question brought her level with me and she did the thing all Tinworth seemed to do, pausing and looking into one's eyes and investing ordinary trivial questions with direct enquiry. As usual it put me slightly at a disadvantage. To say outright that I'd temporarily forgotten that the day before yesterday all the boys and most of the masters had gone home for the summer holidays, and that yesterday the majority of the domestic staff had dispersed also, would be about as silly as mentioning that one had forgotten a recent earthquake or an invasion in arms. On the other hand, if one said that as far as one's own life was concerned it appeared to make no difference at all, I knew a shadow of suppressed excitement would float over that bovine countenance of peaches and cream and she would want to know why. To do it justice, Tinworth never minded asking.

'It's very pleasant,' I said, adding idiotically, 'Are you going to the school?'

'Of course I am. The letters still come, don't they? I should have thought you'd have known that.' There was no impudence in the last observation. It was just another enquiry, a sharp inquisitive enquiry if I'd really forgotten I'd once held down a high-powered secretarial job at St. Jude's Hospital myself. Her blue-eyed stare was filled with pure curiosity. I said nothing at all so she had to go on. 'I expect the Headmaster's out of his room by now, isn't he?'

'He was there when I came out,' I told her, adding drily, 'with Mr. Rorke.'

'Oh.'

I don't know quite how people bridle, but if it means that an expression both disapproving and self-righteous, if admittedly justified, comes over their faces, Maureen bridled.

'I'd better hurry along. Good-bye, Mrs.

Lane.'

The thud of her feet was still in my ears, and I had only just had time to remember that at least she had not asked me outright where we were going for our summer holiday, when I saw my next hurdle. Bickky Seckker was advancing demurely down the path towards me, his gold spectacles glinting in the morning sun.

Mr. P. F. Seckker was senior classics master at Buchanan House, and the fact that he'd been just that for more years than anyone would like to mention probably accounted for much of the school's reputation. His nickname, a reference to his initials, which were the same as those on a favourite brand of shortcake, indicated his standing with successive generations of boys. Very few masters achieve such an innocent soubriquet.

When I first met him I had assumed he was a very ordinary elderly bachelor, a little old-maidish and perhaps the least bit seedy, but as the months went on I had revised my opinion and was fast coming to think he was the kindest soul I had ever met in my life. He smiled at me, hesitated, made sure that I really did want to stop (which I didn't, of course, but I would have died rather than hurt his feelings), and came out with the one most unfortunate remark which from my point of view he could have made.

'I don't know when you're off for your

vacation, Mrs. Lane, but my sister and I will be at home here at Tinworth all the holidays and my sister—I mean we—would be delighted if you'd drop in to see us just whenever you feel like it.' He was a little shy, as he always was with what he was apt to describe quite suddenly as 'a very, very pretty woman,' and he twinkled and glowed at me as if he were twenty-four and not I. 'Nothing formal, you know,' he chattered on. 'We are too old, and like most other people too poor, for formal entertaining, but my sister was talking to you on Speech Day and she thought that, well, you never know, you might care sometime for a cup of tea in our little walled garden.'

He paused abruptly and to my horror I realised that my face was growing scarlet.

'I—I'd love that,' I said. 'I would. I'd like it better than anything. I'm not sure—quite—when we're going away.'

'Naturally.' Now that I had betrayed embarrassment any shyness of his own was thrust aside and he took social command with all the charm and ease of his kind. 'Of course. Well, you must come when you can. We shall be delighted. I love this warm weather. It suits Tinworth. Some people think it's an ugly town, but I don't. We've got history here, you know. The site of the Roman camp at Mildford is perfectly fascinating. I shall show it to you one day. Much better than half the things one travelled all through France to find.' And then, abruptly, as if he were a gauche old person surprised into speech, 'That blue gown of yours makes your dark eyes darker and puts quite a blue light into that black hair of yours. There, isn't that forward of me?'

The old-fashioned word made me laugh, as I think he knew it would.

'No,' I protested. 'It's charming of you. I feel better and younger already.'

'That would be impossible,' he assured me gravely. 'Until I show you the Roman camp, then.' He raised his polished cherry-wood stick in salute, since he was hatless, and strolled on, leaving me shaken to find that even old Miss Seckker, who was considerably his senior and certainly half blind, should have noticed that I might need a little human comfort in the sanctuary of her garden. Yet I was glad I had met him and was grateful for his compliment.

It was at that precise moment as I turned away that I saw Andy. He was speeding down the road towards me in a well-worn open sports car. We looked straight at each other for an instant as he passed and then I heard the shriek of brakes and the revving of the engine as he swung round in the wide road. In the last few hours I suppose I had envisaged meeting him again in half a hundred possible places. For some reason I had assumed that it would be at some very crowded social gathering, the Agricultural Show perhaps, or one of the eternal sherry parties Tinworth likes so much.

I'd even prepared an opening gambit: 'Oh yes, of course I know Dr. Durtham. We met at St. Jude's. How nice to see you again, Andy.'

To find him pulling up beside me in this vast and now apparently empty street called for an entirely different approach and I was so amazed and so pleased to see him that I couldn't think of anything at all suitable.

'Hullo, animal,' I said.

'Hullo yourself,' he said briefly. 'Get in.'

They say it is impossible to forget anyone you've ever been truly in love with, but it is astounding how easy it is to put out of one's mind the things about them which one loved. One of the things I had succeeded in forgetting about Andy Durtham was his force. He was a big, rakish, intensely masculine person, dark as I am and not ill-looking in a tough untidy way, but his chief characteristic, and I suppose charm, was vital energy. It was a bit overwhelming and there had been a period when I had found it alarming. It seemed to radiate from him almost noisily, as if he were an engine ticking over. He was young, of course, only just qualified.

'Get in,' he repeated, holding the door open for me. 'I want to talk to you.'

'I was going to the High Street.'

'Then I'll take you there. Come on, Liz.'

I had been called 'Elizabeth' so thoroughly by this time that I had forgotten how much I disliked the abominable diminutive. It just

12

sounded friendly today. I stepped into the car and he sighed, let in the clutch, and turned round in the road again.

'Hey,' I protested, 'where are you going? I said the High Street.'

'We're going there, by Morton Road and the by-pass. That's the way I know best. I've only been here a week.'

'A week? I didn't know.'

'Too bad. Nobody tells you anything, do they? But I'm going to, and it's going to take me just about seven minutes, so—we'll go by the by-pass.'

I did not speak. Andy was returning to my conscious mind with a rush, and with a new and painful vividness I remembered why I had written to him and not phoned or arranged a meeting when I finally decided to marry Victor.

'Yes, well,' he said, and his mouth twisted down at the corners as it always did when he was embarking on one of his more outrageous performances, 'lean back and relax, because you're going to take this in if it's the last thing I do. I've been thinking about this lecture very thoroughly for some months and here it comes, piping hot.'

He turned and peered at me from under bristling eyebrows.

'First of all, I suppose you know you've lost twenty pounds.'

It was such an unexpected thrust that it took

13

me by surprise. Until that moment I had been enjoying him, like a beautiful draught of fresh air. Now I was annoyed by his impudence.

'Don't be a boor,' I said. 'I've lost eight.'

'They were the eight which held your looks. The wan white waif act doesn't suit you. Don't touch the wheel. You'll break our necks. Still, I'm glad to see you're not completely devitalised in spite of all I've heard since I've been here.'

I had made no real attempt to touch the wheel, of course. I wasn't a child, and we were travelling very fast and passing all the people I'd met before, but I must have stiffened and I felt the blood in my face.

'How extraordinary of you to take this locum job down here,' I said abruptly. 'When did you leave St. Jude's?'

'In my script for this conversation you don't speak.' He was not looking at me. At that moment we were negotiating an unexpectedly narrow turn. The Vicarage car was parked on the corner, as usual, and a milk tanker was attempting to pass. We were held up for a second or two and I found myself face to face with the vicar, who was dithering in front of his aged bonnet with a starting handle. He stared at me, recognised me with open astonishment, and was groping for his hat with his free hand when I was whisked unceremoniously from under his nose.

'You merely listen,' Andy continued,

14

squaring himself as the car leapt forward down the villa-lined length of Morton Road. 'You have made a basic psychological mistake and, having got it clear in my own mind, I intend you to see it. It may not do you much good but you've no idea how it's going to satisfy me! Look, Liz, you never forgave your mother for making a mess of her marriage, did you? You always secretly thought she could have saved it. That's why you made the idiotic mistake of trying to play safe.'

He was speaking with utter sincerity, his tone urgent and forceful, and if instead of speaking he had suddenly pressed a blade directly into my heart I think the pain he gave me must have been exactly the same.

'No,' I said violently, because I wouldn't and couldn't let it be true, 'that's insulting nonsense. For heaven's sake let me get out of here.'

He put on a little more speed and he bounced out into the stream of traffic on the by-pass which Tinworth uses so freely to relieve its own tortuous streets.

'You were in love with me,' he went on doggedly as if I had not spoken. 'Probably you are still, whether you know it or not. But if it's not me someone like me, and it always will be.'

He was not looking at me, which was merciful, for we were in traffic, and he ignored any sound I made but continued the harangue exactly as if I were some recalcitrant patient to whom he was in duty bound to report on a considered diagnosis.

'There's a great deal of rubbish talked about the kind of love I mean,' he said. 'It's sublimated and sublimised and sentimentalised and generally kicked around, but the one ordinary elementary fact which is self-evident is that it is an affinity exactly like a chemical affinity. You know the definition, of that. You must have typed it for old Beaky Bowers at St. Jude's often enough. *'The peculiar attraction between the atoms of two simple substances that makes them combine to form a compound.'* Now I don't suggest that love *is* chemical. I only say that it is *like* it and quite as irrevocable and inescapable. You love something because you need it. It is made up of the things you have not got. You recognise your need instinctively and instinctively you go for it as soon as you find it. Be quiet. Listen. You can get out when I've finished.'

Since I could do nothing else I sat bolt upright, staring in front of me, the furious blood burning in my face. Since I couldn't keep my hat on in that air stream I took it off and held it on my lap. I tried not to listen, either, but one might as well have tried to ignore an avalanche.

'People keep saying that one is attracted by opposites,' Andy's lecture continued, 'but that is one of those sweeping half-truths which are so misleading. What they mean is that if one

16

hasn't got quite enough of a particular characteristic oneself one is automatically attracted by the person who has a little too much of it. When one finds someone who appears to balance out *all* one's own excesses and deficiencies, one falls in love with her—er, or him.'

He turned to me, his vivid grey-blue eyes dark with intelligence, and dropped his professional manner.

'You must know what I mean, Liz. You've got the warmest heart in the world, but with it you tend to be cautious, intellectual and reserved. I tend to be headstrong, intuitive and confiding. You're level-headed to a fault, I'm on the verge of being wild.'

'Wild—' I was beginning, but he stopped me.

'You're overconventional and oversensitive and gentle. I'm basically unconventional and—well, rough. Cruel, if you like.'

Andy's sincerity had always captured me, holding my attention, forcing me to think along lines I would not normally have chosen. It performed its exasperating magic again now.

I was attracted to you, my lad, because you were alive, I thought, and somehow I don't seem to be very much alive alone. There was no point in saying it aloud, of course, and certainly I was alive enough myself at that moment. I was outraged by him. The tastelessness, the utter impropriety, the

17

insolence—all the old-fashioned words crowded onto my tongue, making me temporarily incoherent.

'You happened to need someone like me,' Andy was saying with steady insistence, 'not in spite of my faults but because of them. You couldn't help it.

'At that rate, nor could you.' Of all the words in the world those were the last I had intended to say. They were silly and dangerous, but in the last few seconds he had got under my skin.

'And so what?' He turned his head and I saw his eyes had become as hard as marbles. 'We're not talking about me. I've had my own problem and I've settled it. I sail in three weeks' time. I'm perfectly all right. I'm simply explaining your position to you because I don't think you've seen it.'

'Sail?' I said, as if it were the only word I'd heard. 'Where are you going?'

'Newfoundland. There's a hell of a lot of work to do there. It's a rough, hard, free country and it'll suit me. George Brewster and his wife are going too. She'll have to do the secretarial work for both of us. It'll be hard going but worth it, I think. Anyhow, all that is beside the point. I'm clearing out of the country and I just wanted to explain the whole thing to you before I went. You didn't give me an opportunity at the time and I don't suppose I should have been able to see it so clearly then if you had.'

'There's nothing for you to explain.' My lips felt stiff as I spoke. We were entering the lower end of the High Street and I gathered my hat and basket with what I felt was a gesture of finality. 'I had merely made up my mind what I thought would be the best for both of us.'

'You'd done nothing of the sort, you know, Liz.' Instead of pulling in to the curb he put on a burst of speed which shot us out into the main stream of the morning shopping traffic. I saw several faces I recognised, all of them surprised, but I had no time even to acknowledge them. Andy proceeded to wind his way expertly through the throng of familiar cars, talking all the time in his forceful, forthright way.

'I had a night out with the boys, got in a stupid rag, and finished up at a police station. There was a row at the hospital and I got an imperial raspberry,' he was saying cheerfully. 'It wasn't very clever of me, but it's a thing that happens to young doctors who haven't left medical school quite long enough. It did me no harm, probably a bit of good in the long run because it scared me and showed me I wasn't quite as intelligent as I thought I was. But the harm it did, the real harm, Liz, was that it frightened you.'

I made an inarticulate noise but he took no notice of it.

'It frightened you out of all reason, all proportion,' he said. 'I ought to have understood it and been prepared for it, but I wasn't. You've grown up obsessed by the broken marriage of your parents which spoilt your childhood, and you were determined not to make the same mistake. Therefore, when you saw yourself as you thought in love with a drunken ne'er-do-well (I'm not blaming you, woman, I'm simply clarifying your mind for you) you panicked, and to save yourself from love you took a safe offer which happened to come along at that particular moment.'

'If you'll stop I'll get out,' I said.

'Can't park on the corner. Besides, I haven't finished. We'll go round again. This is the last time I shall ever speak to you and I intend to get this right off my chest.'

We swept out of the main street towards the Tortham Road again and I was suddenly glad. If this was to be a once-and-forever fight I had something to say myself. It welled up inside me in a great wave of self-justification. It was the thing I'd been wanting to explain to the whole of Tinworth—to the world for that matter—for solid months.

'I married as I did because I was determined to make a success of it,' I bellowed, and, realising I was shouting, lowered my voice abruptly. 'You're quite right, in one sense,' I went on, trying to sound reasonable and succeeding only in conveying my savage irritation. 'I did remember Mother. I did remember how a romantic love affair had become a jealous bickering match. I did remember that love can die and a woman and her child can be reduced to dreary misery in the process. I didn't want that kind of marriage. I didn't want the humiliation of any more divorces. Mother's was enough for me. I did remember all that, and therefore I married where I felt I could make a good honest job of it. I wanted to be a good wife and I wanted to stay married. Now do you understand?'

He did not answer immediately and when I looked at him his head was turned a little so that I could only see the angle of his jaw. His face was darker than ever and I was very much aware of the hard angry muscles under the coat sleeve at my side. We were roaring up Tortham Road again by this time and he did not speak until we swung round past the Vicarage once more. Then he said mildly:

'Then it wasn't altogether the row?'

'No, of course it wasn't. That simply cleared my mind, and, as you said, Victor happened to come along at the same moment.' I felt I was gaining my point and couldn't understand why it didn't make me feel happier.

Andy brought the car to a crawl and looked at me curiously.

'You just honestly don't see it, do you, Liz?' He made the observation almost gently. 'You don't want to, of course. That's why you're deceiving yourself. You were afraid of love, old lady, that's what you were escaping from. You wanted something safer.'

His stupidity and obstinacy made me absolutely furious. I had never felt so helpless. For three quarters of a year I had been clarifying my mind in private upon the subject, until I felt I knew all about everything I had ever felt or ever could feel. Now, when I tried to express it for the first time to another human being, it seemed to be going all wrong. To make matters worse, until that moment I should have said that Andy was the easiest person in the world to whom to tell anything. It was his greatest gift, both as a doctor and as a man.

'Look here,' I said, making what I felt was a last attempt to get through the wool, 'call it an ideal, if you like. I had set my heart on a steady, sober, ordinary sort of marriage, something I could make something of.'

'And have you got it?'

The question came out quite naturally and without the least hint of malice. It hit me, of course. I felt the blood go hot in my face. It rose into my hair, making the roots tingle.

'I think so,' I said. 'I mean, of course I have.' There was a pause and I added idiotically, 'Term time is liable to be very busy for Victor.'

He cocked a shrewd eye at me and I realised all over again how very well we two were acquainted. It wasn't going to be easy to hide much from Andy.

'And you haven't had much except term time so far, have you?' he was saying slowly. 'As I hear it, you were married just two days before the spring term began. Your husband had to spend a short vacation at the end of that term on a course at a Swiss university where you couldn't accompany him. And now here you are at the end of the summer session and he's due to go on a mountain-climbing expedition—experts only.'

This shook me and I showed it. I couldn't help it. My mouth fell open. For the past twelve hours or so I had thought that I was the only person to know about this latest bombshell of Victor's, but if Andy had picked up the information in the week he'd been in Tinworth it seemed I was rather late off the mark. I was so amazed I forgot to be humiliated. Some sort of preservative sixth sense was working, however, and I spoke promptly.

'Victor has explained. That was arranged a long time ago. You seem to know a great deal about us.'

'Only what everybody tells me.' He gave me a sudden disarming grin. 'This is my first experience of a provincial town. You seem to have got yourself in a fine old parrot house, ducky. They're wonderful, aren't they? Every man his own detective. No mystery too small! Do you *like* them, Liz?'

'I don't know any of them very well, yet,' I said evasively. 'They're all right. Not terribly exciting.' My mind was beginning to work again. I told myself it was all very unfortunate meeting Andy, and he was behaving abominably, but here was a chance to find out exactly where I did stand with the town. At least I knew him well enough to know he wouldn't lie. I began with great caution. 'There isn't much outside entertainment in a place like this,' I said. 'People talk about their neighbours because there isn't much else to interest them. Sometimes they get things rather wrong.' I hesitated. He didn't speak. 'I don't know what you've heard about me?'

'About you?'

'Well, about us generally. What is the gossip? You seem to have the impression that there is some. Let me straighten it out for you.'

He had the grace to look uncomfortable but to my relief he didn't avoid the direct question.

'There's no gossip, exactly.' He bent forward to push a bundle of untidy memo slips and prescription pads back in the locker in the dashboard, so that I could only see his cheek. It had coloured a little. 'There's no "talk", old girl, nothing to worry about.'

'No, but what do they actually say?'

'Oh, they're only intrigued,' he said at last.

'About Victor's marriage? Do they mind him marrying? Do they object to a city girl?'

'Oh no, no, nothing like that. You've got it

24

wrong, Liz.' He was looking at me earnestly now, desperately anxious not to be clumsy and hating being involved. I knew it served him right but I was almost sorry for him.

'Well?' I persisted.

'It's the setup which they find so interesting,' he began at last. 'This husband of yours is a well-known local man who for years seemed set to remain a bachelor. He seems to have run his life and his school to a very firmly fixed schedule. The school runs like a machine and his own holidays have followed the same hidebound pattern. At week ends he plays golf hard and actually has a cottage near the links to save time. On the Easter vacation he goes on some university course designed to fill it. In the long summer holiday he goes on an expedition up a mountain with a team of which he is the president, and at Christmas he has a three weeks' cultural whirl in London or Paris. Tinworth knew all about his programme and was used to it.'

He eyed me to see if I was agreeing with him and I made my face impassive.

'Well,' he went on, 'think of it. One day this lad turns up with a beautiful young wife who appears to have been something of an organiser herself, and who looks and sounds as if she might have some ideas of her own. Naturally everyone sits up waiting to see the changes.' He paused and gave me one of his shrewder stares. 'As far as they can see, there haven't been any changes. He seems to be living exactly the same sort of—well, somewhat self-absorbed life he always did. Tinworth is dying to know what you're making of it, that's all.'

It was his tone on the last two words which made me look up. Until then he had told me nothing that I did not know rather too well, except that I had not realised that Tinworth saw things quite so clearly; but something in that last little phrase struck an alarm bell in my mind.

'It sounds as if it wasn't all,' I murmured, and added, 'You never were any good at hiding things.'

'I'm not hiding anything.' He spoke a trifle too loudly but a settled obstinacy had spread over his face and I knew I should get nothing more out of him. 'I've said too much anyway,' he insisted. 'I was merely trying to point out that although your neighbours down here do seem to be a pack of chatty old geese, I don't think they're entirely unreasonable. After all, people always do sit round a marriage and watch who wins, that's natural.'

'They think I'm losing, I suppose?'

'They think you needn't lie down under the steam roller and quite frankly neither do I. There's no need to lose all that weight, surely? And usen't your hair to have a wave in it—at the sides, I mean?'

That did it. It was that bit of silly masculine

clumsiness coming just at the right moment which saved me from going to pieces and telling him the whole story. I might so easily have tried to explain what it felt like to drop feet foremost into just such a machine as he had described, and just how impossible it was to reason with or to cajole a man who never had a moment to hear one. I might also have indulged in the bad taste of recounting what happened when one tried to stage a full-scale row, as I had on the evening before when the news that 'of course' the alpine expedition would take place as usual had been given me so casually. I might also have dilated upon the difference between a man who is merely cold and one who seemed to have nothing to be warm with . . . a man one couldn't even make angry. As it was, I was so hurt I said nothing whatever.

Andy turned the car slowly into the High Street again and edged slowly in to the curb.

'It hasn't turned out as I meant it to,' he said abruptly. 'I've been obsessed with the desire to get things off my chest, and now that I've done it it doesn't seem to have got us anywhere. Honestly, I didn't just want to add to any difficulties you may have, Liz.' He was silent for a moment and then said awkwardly, with the idea of making amends, no doubt, 'I think you'll like to know that nobody blames you for the whirlwind courtship. This fellow, he—er, your husband, has tremendous charm and drive, they say . . .'

By this time I was shaking with some emotion which I vaguely supposed was anger. I heard myself cutting in with a very stupid and revealing statement:

'At least the confirmed bachelor did ask me to marry him, Andy. In all the excitement over our private affairs, no one seems to have offered an explanation for that rather important point.' I was looking full at Andy as I spoke and I saw his expression. He looked suddenly guilty. So the gossips had a neat little explanation for that too, had they? Whatever it was, he was not repeating it. He hopped out of the car and came round to open the door for me. Standing on the pavement, we shook hands very formally. 'Good-bye Andy,' I said. 'I don't suppose I'll see you again.'

He stood looking down at me gloomily and there was nothing but emptiness all round us.

'No,' he said at last, 'no, Liz, I don't suppose you will. Sorry about all this. Silly of me. Good-bye, old lady, good luck.'

We each turned away abruptly at the same moment and I walked off down the crowded pavement, unaware what I looked like and without seeing anyone at all. Yet when I reached the chain store on the corner I went in and bought myself one of those cheap home perm outfits. It was something of a gesture because Victor suggested all beauty treatments a waste of time and slightly vulgar, and I had

28

had no money to spare for them since my marriage.

I was standing in the queue at the cash desk, still feeling as if there was a good stiff layer of ice between me and the rest of the world, when Hester Raye pounced upon me.

There may be Hester Rayes in other parts of the earth, but she has always seemed to me to belong quite peculiarly to a certain small section of present-day society in southern England. Her husband, Colonel Raye, was Chief Constable of the county (the police always seem to choose a retired army man to command them) and she herself had sprung from army stock. At fifty she was still good-looking. Neither time nor experience had bequeathed her any tact whatever, and her intense interest in other people did not seem to have taught her anything important about them at all. She ploughed through the small-town life of Tinworth like an amiable tank.

Her smiling eyes, which looked so misleadingly intelligent, shone into mine.

'Buying yourself something to make you look pretty? That's right, never give up. I never have.' It was a typical pronouncement, guaranteed at best to be misunderstood, and at the same moment she gave my arm a squeeze which would have startled a bear. 'I was talking about you only the other day to someone—I forget who, but it was someone quite intelligent—and I said then I did hope

29

you wouldn't let your husband dry all the life and youth out of you—for you're quite beautiful, you know; you are really when you take trouble—but that you'd stand up to him and get a little life of your own however selfish he is. He's *so* charming, isn't he, and *such* a villain . . .'

I had heard her talk as frankly as this to other acquaintances and I had wondered how on earth one responded to the bland, patronising gush which yet had a sort of outrageous bonhomie in it. Now I understood the fishlike stares which I had observed on the faces of her victims. There was no protection one could devise against her at all. She was a product of the twenties, when it had been fashionable to say the unforgivable thing, and like the little girl who grimaced in the nursery story, the wind had changed and she had stayed like it. I remember thinking vaguely that it was quite clear that she meant well, and perhaps that was why no one had ever gone berserk and killed her.

'Are you going back now?' she demanded. 'Because if you are I'll give you a lift. I've got the car outside. I've often seen you walking down Tortham Road and I've said, "I bet he doesn't even let that sweet girl drive his car in the morning." No, don't run away. I want to make you promise you'll come to the Flower Club meeting tomorrow. I've gone to fantastic lengths to get Judith Churchman down to lecture on the modern trend in flower decoration, and I just must have a big audience. You did promise, you know.'

'I'll be there.' I realised I had shouted at her a second too late to do anything about it. The avalanche of dropped bricks had been too much for me altogether. I must have looked rather wild as well, for to my dismay she decided I was having a nerve storm.

'Oh, you poor child,' she said, her grip on me tightening. 'Come along. I insist. I'll drive you home. You're terribly brave to put such a good face on things, you know. Everybody says so.'

'Then I think everybody's making rather a silly mistake.' I walked along beside her as I spoke and climbed into her car. There had been more cold venom in my tone than I thought I could summon and I noted her startled expression with deep satisfaction. 'People who discuss couples whom they don't know at all often make utter and rather offensive fools of themselves, don't you think?'

She did not answer. The colour had come into her face and she made a great business of starting up and getting out into the traffic. However, I had reckoned without her powers of resilience. Before we had gone fifty yards she was herself again.

'You don't know how you surprised me or how pleased I am,' she announced with gay naïveté. 'We'd all been pitying you, you know.

Wasn't it dreadful of us? I expect it'll make you furious, but it's terribly funny really. Of course we've all known Victor for years, that's why. You've got him right under your thumb, have you? Good for you, my dear. He's going to give up that old summer expedition and take you somewhere, is he?'

'He's not going on the expedition.' The words came out with a conviction which was completely unjustified, particularly in view of the few chill words Victor and I had had on the subject the evening before. Victor never had a row. That was one of the few things I had come to learn about him so painfully in the past few months. He simply stated his intention. Usually that was enough. However, as soon as I spoke to Mrs. Raye that morning I realised that I had started some intentions too, and I knew that the expedition would have to be the issue which settled things between me and Victor for good and all. She gave me an odd little glance and I met it steadily, in fact our eyes watched each other until hers dropped. After a while she giggled.

'My dear, how wonderful! Just to see you about, you know, one wouldn't dream that you had it in you. You sounded positively sinister.' She laughed; as far as I could tell with genuine amusement, and settled down to be cosily confidential. 'This really is quite terrific and I'm terribly glad because we've all been thinking that it was rather mean of Victor getting married suddenly like that to silence all the talk, but then we never realised you *knew*. We all thought that you were the complete little innocent, you see.'

She was watching the road ahead and did not see my face, which was fortunate. She drove with the same calm effrontery with which she seemed to conduct her social life, and while she forced her way through a bunch of traffic I had time to grasp what she was telling me.

Victor's sudden decision to find a wife had been occasioned by his desperate need to silence some sort of gossip which threatened, presumably, his position at the school. That was the part of the story which Andy had forborne to mention. I knew it was true as soon as Mrs. Raye spoke. It explained so much about Victor and my life with him, and made so clear and even forgivable the attitude of the townsfolk towards me. So that was it. That was the solution of the one mystery which, until now, had given me some sort of justification, some sort of hope for my ridiculous ideal for a safe, sound marriage, based on something more solid than the dangerous sands of love. Now I could see exactly the sort of fool I'd been.

To my relief I discovered that I was quite past feeling hurt. I had had more than I could take already that morning, and now I found myself in that quiet grey country which is on the other side of pain. I was hard and uncharacteristically shrewd and quick-witted.

'Oh, I think any bachelor in a small town like this is hopelessly vulnerable to gossip,' I remarked lightly, 'but I hardly see poor Victor as the local Don Juan, I'm afraid.' In my tone there was just enough contempt for the wild life of Tinworth to arouse her. I found that once one decided to pull no punches she was almost simple to manage. She rose to the bait at once.

'Oh, don't you be so sure,' she said, quite forgetting who I was, apparently, in her anxiety to make her point. 'He's been awfully well behaved lately, of course, but *last winter* . . .! I Well, there never is any smoke without fire, is there? Besides, you can't tell *me*. What about that little hidey-hole he has out on the road to Latchenden?'

'The cottage by the golf course?' I said wonderingly.

'Golf course!' she exploded. 'What other man wants a cottage to play golf in?'

It occurred to me that she had something there and that either I'd been born blind or was ripe for the half-wit home. But to do Victor justice, I'd been shown over the place, which was a very primitive little affair, and had understood it was merely an escape from the school for an occasional semi-camping week end. I knew he'd lent it to a couple of masters once or twice during term, and it had been used for school picnics. It had certainly never struck me as being anything in the light of a love nest. But now that she mentioned it, I could see that it was perhaps a rather odd place for him to possess, little more than a couple of miles out of the town.

'What is he supposed to take up there?' I demanded. 'Strings of dancing girls?'

I suppose the bitterness showed through. Anyway, it was not an intelligent thing to have said, for she gave me a sudden wary glance and began to retract, stumbling over herself in her anxiety.

'Oh, I'm not saying there was anything wrong, my dear. I only spoke of the talk, and how grateful he must be to you that that's all died down. Tinworth isn't narrow-minded. After all, none of us are saints, are we?'

She gave me a roguish smile which belonged all to the 1920s and pulled up beside the school gates.

'I thought *your* boy friend was very handsome this morning, for instance. Had you met him before? You seemed to be getting along very well.'

She caught me off guard and I felt my expression growing horror-stricken. She laughed outright at that and touched my arm.

'Round and round the town, every time one came out of a shop there you were tearing down the road with your heads together. You can't say you don't know who I mean. He's

35

doing a locum for Dr. Browning, isn't he? Somebody pointed you both out to me this morning and said so, I forgot who. Well, don't cut the Flower lecture tomorrow, will you? So long, my dear, and I shall tell everybody that we were quite wrong about you. I think you're quite wonderful . . .'

The car slid away without my having to say anything at all, which was merciful in the circumstances.

*   *   *

The rose-red buildings looked forbidding and forlorn as schools do out of term time. The shaven grass was well worn and although there was no litter or untidiness about, yet the place had all the shabby sadness of a deserted nursery. I walked along the side path, aware of the heat haze and of the loneliness but principally conscious that I had no place there. This was not my home. However much I tried, it would never have room for me.

I passed under the main arch which had been constructed through the house into the quadrangle behind without seeing a soul, but instead of going straight to the Headmaster's Lodging, which was in the centre of the block on the southern side, I passed by it and went on to the narrow gate behind the chapel. I had got to have things out once and for all with Victor, but I wanted to be quite sure of myself first. There must be no tears or other signs of hysteria in that interview, and I needed a little more time to collect myself.

Behind the chapel lay all those utility buildings, old and new, which did not fit into the main architectural scheme. The boiler houses were there, and the glasshouses and the swimming pool, the disused stables and the laundries, all huddled together in a fine muddle of old elegance and new necessity. I went into the stables and as my footstep sounded on the bricks there was a single shrill bark from the further loose-box. Izzy was in my arms a moment later, bounding up on his short legs, his hard brindled body wriggling in ecstasy. This wild greeting nearly broke my heart, it was so uncharacteristic of his dour Scotty personality. A year before he would never have lowered his dignity by anything more than a discreet wagged tail at my arrival, but then at that time we had never been apart during his lifetime. This kennel business was part of Victor's discipline. He had been very nice about it but very firm. I had seen that if the boys were not allowed pets in the school I could hardly expect to have mine at large, and so very comfortable quarters were arranged for Izzy and I took him for walks every day. It was very nice, but just not our idea of life, that was all. Poor Izzy and poor Liz, both victims of the same silly mistake. However, this was the end of all that. I had decided it.

I set Izzy down and left the door of the box wide.

'Come on,' I said, 'you get a bath after lunch. You smell like a dog.'

He peered at me from under his fierce old-man eyebrows and the little black eyes which had earned him his pet name were shining and hopeful. He bounded a little, very clumsily as Scotch terriers do, and then parked himself at my heels in complete content. Where I was going, so was he. I felt much better with him behind me.

We came back together and were crossing the yard when the door of the shower room, which was next to the pool, was shattered open and a most unexpected person came reeling out almost on top of us. It took me a moment or two to recognise Mr. Rorke, our much-discussed science master. It was generally understood that Rorke, although admittedly brilliant, possessed what was euphemistically described as an 'unfortunate failing.' Until now I had never taken the story seriously. I had only seen the gaunt white-faced scarecrow of a man at meals in the dining hall, and perhaps twice at the dreary functions which were described as the 'Headmaster's coffee party,' and then he had seemed to me to be a harmless and even a pathetic figure. I had supposed somewhat vaguely that his transgressions took the form of quiet tippling in the secrecy of his room, and was quite unprepared for this spectacular performance so early in the day. Moreover, he appeared to have attempted to remedy matters by taking a shower, at least from the waist upwards, but as he had omitted to remove even his jacket for the operation his condition now was pitiful. I never saw a man in such a mess. His hair hung over his eyes in a damp mess and he was shaking violently. Izzy drew back and began to growl and I hesitated, uncertain whether it would be kindest to offer assistance or to ignore him altogether. To my dismay he paused directly in my path and shook a wavering acid-stained hand at me.

'You too,' he shouted, 'you too.'

I did not quite gather the rest of the sentence. It sounded as if he prophesied that I should or should not be sorry, I was not sure which.

'You go and change and lie down,' I commanded, summoning all the authority I could muster. 'You'll feel better.' But my tolerance faded suddenly and the smile was wiped off my face.

Through his tousled hair his eyes peered at me with an intensity which was intelligent and menacing. I drew back involuntarily and he swung away and lurched off down the yard towards the back gates. I looked after him, wondering if I ought not to do something to see he came to no harm, or if it would be unwise to interfere. Izzy settled the matter by prodding me firmly in the ankle with his wet nose. It was one of his most characteristic gestures and meant 'get along out of here.' It reminded me that I had troubles of my own to attend to, so I collected myself and went along to the Lodging to find Victor.

As Izzy and I entered the light, white-painted hall where the parquet shone with hygienic cleanliness, the silence of the building descended on me like a tangible cloak. In the normal way the house was full of hurrying people, and the chatter of typewriters from the school office never seemed to cease. But all was quiet now and still in the sunlight. It was a queer little dwelling, designed for its purpose by the architect who had converted the mansion. On the ground floor there were two rooms, one on either side of the square hall. One was the office, the other was the Headmaster's study. On the floor above was a drawing room for the Headmaster's entertaining, a very small dining room, a bachelor bedroom and bath. One floor higher still was a little suite of three rooms for the use, presumably, of any family the Headmaster might want to tuck away up there. Until my arrival it had been deserted. Now I lived there, for the most part of the time alone. There was no housekeeping. We came under school management. The school servants kept the house clean. We fed in hall with the boys during the day, and in the evenings our meal

40

was sent up from the school kitchens and served with due ceremony by the head steward. Victor had always lived like that and had seemed horrified when, early in the present term, I had suggested that I might instal a small kitchen of my own. I suppose I ought to have put my foot down over some of these points, but when one is fighting against the conviction that one had made a really big mistake, one is apt to be unduly cautious about making small ones, so I had concentrated on trying to make a go of things, on fitting in and giving way. It had got me exactly nowhere. I was getting that into my head at last.

Well, if it was to be settled once and for all, the sooner the better. I pulled myself together and walked into the study. I did not knock, as I usually did in case Victor was interviewing somebody. Term was over and I was in my own house.

But there was no one at the big desk which spread so importantly over the far half of the carpet. The tall windows draped with formal curtains were closed. The room was airless and deserted. It was anticlimax and I was turning to go out again when a smothered gasp from the fireplace on my left brought me wheeling round towards it.

Mr. Seckker was kneeling on the hearthrug, surprised in the very act of burning something in the empty grate, for a thin blue wand of smoke still wavered up the chimney as I

41

looked. For a second he stared at me, dismay on his prim wrinkled face, but he recovered himself at once and hopped up with quite remarkable agility to stand smiling at me with all his wonted courtliness, although he took care, I noticed, to step between me and the fireplace.

'Oh, it's you, Mrs. Lane,' he said easily. 'I thought for a moment it was the Headmaster returning. I don't know that I shall wait for him after all. I can come up tomorrow.'

'Is Victor out?' I said in surprise. 'I've just come back from the town. I didn't meet him.'

'Then he must have gone the other way, mustn't he?' he said, twinkling at me. 'I was in my classroom and I saw him drive out of the gates—when was that? Let me see, half an hour ago perhaps. I came in here to bring him some books and settled down to wait with my pipe. I flicked a match into the grate and I'm afraid I set light to some litter which was there. I was just seeing it was all right when you came in.'

He made the unnecessary explanation with bland charm and even waved a palpably empty pipe at me by the way of corroboration. I nodded absently. Whatever he was doing, it had nothing to do with me. I was thinking of Victor.

'You don't know where he's gone, do you?' I said. 'I mean, he'll be in to lunch, won't he?'

'I really don't know.' He looked astounded

at my ignorance and faintly disapproving. I realised that Mr. Seckker's sister knew to the hour and second when her brother would be in to a meal. 'I've not seen him myself this morning. He was closeted in here with Rorke when I arrived and so I went up to my classroom. Then I saw him go out. Dear me, it's past twelve. I must get back.'

He glanced behind him at the fireplace with misleading casualness and, seeing, no doubt, that all was well, came across the room to me. As he passed I suddenly remembered.

'Oh yes,' I said, 'Mr. Rorke. I suppose he'll be okay?'

'All right?' He stopped in his tracks and stared at me with sudden sternness. 'What do you mean by that?'

I told him of my encounter in the stable yard and as he listened I got the impression that he was relieved rather than scandalised.

'Wet, was he?' he said, laughing a little in a dour, elderly way. 'Oh yes, he'll be all right, silly fellow. Don't give him another thought, Mrs. Lane. Good morning.' Halfway across the hall he glanced back. 'Please don't bother the Headmaster with any message from me. I may or may not drop in tomorrow. The matter I was going to mention to him is of no importance.' Without actually saying so he made me realise that it was a definite request and I said, 'I won't, then.'

He still hesitated and finally added, with a

diffidence which was quite charming: 'Unless you feel you ought, I don't think I should bother him about Rorke either. He's a silly young juggins, but it's not strictly term time, although he was on school premises . . .'

'Of course,' I said. 'I shouldn't dream of mentioning it to him.'

'Ah.' It was a satisfied little sound. He gave me a nod which was almost a bow, and pattered off, letting himself quietly out of the house and closing the door behind him. I started upstairs, the little brindled shadow which was Izzy close at my heels, and smiled at his description of Rorke, who must have been close on the to me impossible age of forty if I was any judge at all. The sudden vista of years all to be spent in the aridity of Buchanan House took me by surprise, and to my dismay I felt if not a scream at least a protesting squeak rising up in my throat. I blushed at myself. Things were getting me down further than I had supposed. I realised this afresh when Izzy's low growl behind me made me start so violently that I almost stepped on him.

'What is it, boy?' I said, and at the same moment I heard from above us the clatter of footsteps on the parquet of the dining room, and the school housekeeper, Miss Richardson, came bustling out onto the landing.

'Oh, there you are, Mrs. Lane,' she said. 'I'm so glad to have caught you. I thought I should have to go without saying goodbye, and

I did want to tell you what I've arranged.'

I stared at her. In all my time at the school I don't suppose we had exchanged half a dozen words. In the very beginning Victor had made it clear to me that one of the dangers of my position at the school was that the domestic staff, who were the employees of the governors, might suspect me of intrusion, with the result, of course, that I had avoided any contact with them. I'm afraid I had hardly dared recognise this plump middle-aged woman, with her strings of domestic science diplomas, as an ordinary human being. I had passed her occasionally in the grounds, looking very aloof in her black skirt and twin set, and we had shown our teeth at each other in polite mirthless smiles. Now I scarcely recognised her in a pale grey linen suit with a white flower on her lapel and a smart white straw set pertly on her glossy dark hair. She had a warm voice, I noticed for the first time, and, now that she was in holiday mood, real gaiety in her smile.

'I couldn't find you anywhere this morning, and the Headmaster was engaged, so I couldn't ask when you were going off,' she rattled on. 'I was a bit worried, but I've done what I think will suit you. Williams will be caretaking all through the holiday . . .'

'That's the porter.'

She looked at me as if I were demented. 'Yes, you know, the man at the lodge. He'll be there all the vacation and he'll have the keys.

Mrs. Williams is always very anxious to help, and if you should come back at any time you can always send her a card and she'll get the place aired and have a meal for you. But I was really worrying about the next day or so before you go. I've fixed up for Mrs. Veal, who is the best of our charwomen, to come in tomorrow morning to see what you need. I've had some cold lunch laid here now, and if you'll just leave everything she'll see to it . . .'

Her voice trailed away and died before the expression on my face, which I suppose was utterly blank.

'You did *know*, I suppose?' she demanded abruptly.

It was one of those purely feminine questions which seem to have 'I thought so' lingering somewhere in their depths, and it pulled me together at once.

'If you mean, had I realised that the whole of the staff was going on holiday today, I'm afraid I hadn't,' I said, trying to sound easy and casual, as if minor items of this kind meant nothing to me. 'I was thinking of last vacation.'

'Oh, but that was Easter, the short vac. We don't bother to disrupt the working arrangements for three weeks or so. But this is a long holiday, nearly nine weeks.'

'Yes, yes, of course,' I said hurriedly. 'Well, thank you tremendously. I'll look out for Mrs. Veal and . . .'

'How long do you expect to stay here, Mrs.

Lane?' She was watching me with black-fringed candid eyes.

'I—I'm not sure at the moment.'

She did not seem to hear me but went on as though she had made up her mind to say something and was going through with it at all costs.

'I asked because some weeks ago when I mentioned the holidays to the Headmaster he told me that he would be going off to the Continent almost immediately the term ended, and that you would probably leave at the same time to stay with friends in London. That's why I haven't consulted you before. Do believe me, Mrs. Lane, it wasn't until last night, when I realised that you hadn't made any arrangements yet—about travelling, I mean—that I began to worry how you'd get on. This morning I tried to find you, but when I discovered I'd missed you I went ahead and made the best arrangements I could.'

'It was very kind of you,' I said, and meant it.

'Not at all. I feel terrible about it.' She gave up all pretences and was appealing to me for my confidence. 'I wish I'd known you weren't going off somewhere at once. I'd have done anything, I would really. I'd have stayed myself.'

'Don't be silly,' I said cheerfully. 'You go and catch your train and have a wonderful time. Where are you going?'

'Devon,' she said, and made it sound like a prayer. Then she caught my eye and actually blushed, so that I got a glimpse of fuchsia hedges and bowls of clotted cream and someone waiting for her, no doubt.

She glanced at her watch and fled, but at the bottom of the stairs she looked back.

'You'll have to order some milk,' she called up to me. 'Mrs. Veal will get it if you tell her how much you want. Good-bye.'

The door closed behind her and the house became so quiet that even the warm sunlight seemed eerie. I had never known a place to feel quite so empty. I sat down on the top step of the stairs because I happened to be standing there, and Izzy sat beside me. My first thought was that it wasn't true. 'Men don't behave like that,' I said aloud. But they do to their wives, said a voice in my mind. Don't be silly; you read it every day in the newspapers. Besides, it's so like Victor, isn't it? Just quietly arranging to get his own way without considering anyone else in the world. Victor doesn't get involved in arguments or explanations. He just fixes up to avoid giving any. Sometimes he goes to considerable lengths in this direction, getting married for instance. By all accounts that must have avoided one father and mother of an argument.

I felt myself growing very hot and presently I got up slowly and mounted the stairs to my own rooms. Sitting before my dressing table, I looked dispassionately at the pale, thin-faced creature in the glass until I awoke a gleam of courage in her eyes. After a while we even laughed at each other.

'Well, he'll be in for lunch in a minute and this is the one argument he isn't going to avoid, my dear,' I said. 'I'd go and get a rolling pin—if we had a kitchen.'

That was just before one o'clock. By a quarter past three it had become evident that wherever Victor was lunching it wasn't at home. He'd side-stepped again, very neatly, very completely. It was typical.

Izzy and I had some of the cold food which Miss Richardson had so kindly left for us, and afterwards I stacked the two plates and left them on the minute sideboard and tidied the table. There was nowhere to wash up unless one used the bathroom.

By this time I had begun to hate myself and the house even more, so I thought I'd walk it off. Just round the school the fields were dull and highly cultivated but about half a mile farther down the road there was a lane that led to the water meadows which cradled our local river. It would be cool down there and lonely, I thought, a good place to think things out and get myself reorientated. Everyone in Tinworth who was not actually infirm owned a bicycle and I was no exception. I got it out of the shed next to the stable where Izzy had lived so long

49

and put him in the basket. He was too big for it and he made the handlebars wobble, but his legs were rather short for fast running and the main road was very hard for his pads. He was used to this form of transport, so he sat very still, his ears flat, and tried, I was certain, to adjust his weight to the balance. One of the gardeners was sweeping near the back gates and he swung them open for us. I saw his surprise as we appeared and his grin as we passed him. Taking advantage of the pause, he pulled a watch out of his pocket and glanced at it to see how much more he had of the afternoon. It was an insignificant incident. I don't know why I noticed it.

There was very little traffic on the high road and once we entered the lane we did not see a soul. I rode on until the going became too rough, and afterwards left the bike in the hedge and walked on to the stile. Izzy was delighted and showed it in his own sedate way, by taking short meaningless runs through the lush grass, his head ploughing up and down through the green as if he were swimming.

It was Andy who, long before in a London park, had pointed out that Izzy was like a very small old-fashioned railway engine, squat, rusty and quite incredibly heavy. I smiled at the recollection and dismissed it hastily. I was determined to put Andy right out of my mind. He had loved me and I had jilted him and he had got over it. That was all there was to that story and to think about it now would be to complicate things quite unbearably.

'I did love you once.' The line from *Hamlet* came back unbidden, the most cruel thing man had ever said to woman, my English mistress had once remarked in a moment of uncharacteristic self-revelation. A whole classful of girls had gaped at her, but she had been right. I knew it now. Andy had said that, almost in as many words, and he'd made it worse by not even meaning to be unkind. I did not blame him. I was just going to forget him, that was all.

I wandered on beside the running water and Izzy puffed and grunted beside me. It was a glorious afternoon, sleepy and golden, and I discovered that I was being careful to think only of immediate things, like the moorhen I disturbed or the lark I tried to see high in the white-flecked blue. It would not do. There was one vital issue I had got to face and the sooner the better if I was going to have it out with Victor. Was it to be divorce, or was I going to sit down under this slow-starvation marriage for the rest of my life?

I lay down on the bank where the turf was short and let my hand dangle in the water, and Izzy came and sat beside me, panting, until he found how to get his nose down to lap. Theoretically the thing was perfectly simple. I had made a hash of getting married and the sensible thing to do was to cut my losses and

51

clear out and get a job. Any civilised young woman of the Western Hemisphere surely knew that by this time. Yet now that I was up against the reality I found there was a remarkable difference between knowing and doing. It may have been just the failure I didn't want to face. Everybody, all my friends, anyone who had ever known me, knew that I was unreasonably terrified of divorce. What Andy had said about me was true. Mother's divorce had coloured my entire outlook from babyhood, and now, although I saw my foolishness, I also saw that one couldn't alter oneself just by knowing one was silly. I still hoped to cling to the crazy idea that somehow I could make it come all right. All the same . . . Victor would never alter. That was the conviction I'd been fighting off for weeks. People don't alter. They may with enormous difficulty modify themselves, but they never really change. I'd got myself married to an overbearing selfish man with a masterful personality, and unless I got away from him he'd reduce me to the colourless cipher he needed as a front-of-the-house wife.

But, there again . . . was it to easy to *get* a divorce? This was England, not one of those countries where a thoroughly unhappy marriage is considered to be, by and large, fair ground for an appeal. If Victor did not help, and I did not think he would for a moment, then I might easily merely provoke a scandal which would ruin his career and leave me tied to him irrevocably for the rest of my life . . . or his.

Oh, dear God, I thought, it is difficult, too difficult. I put my head down in the warm grass and shut out everything from my mind but the sound of the gently lapping water. The sun was warm on my back. Izzy waddled over and settled his hard little body against my shoulder. The river sang softly, lipperty-lapperty, lipperty-lapperty . . . .

I woke cold and stiff, and astounded to find it was nearly dusk. Doubtless it was the air, following all the emotional upset, which had put me out. At any rate, I had slept deeply and dreamlessly for heaven knows how long and might have stayed there half the night had not Izzy's patience given out. He prodded my ear gently until I sat up and stared about me. Even if one has nothing in the world to do, one feels guilty at dropping off to sleep unintentionally, and I got up in a fine hurry and set off back to the stile and the bicycle with as much haste as if I had a nurseryful of youngsters to feed. I had no idea what the time was but when we reached the high road one of the cars which passed us had its sidelights on.

I had guessed the back gates of the school would be closed, but the big main ones in front were locked also and I had to rouse Williams in his lodge beside them to get in. He was astonished to see me, and apologetic.

'I thought we was on our own, me and the missis,' he said, his little bright eyes peering at me from out of a mass of wrinkles. 'Thought you'd all gorn. The Guv'nor's out, you know. Leastways, his car ain't in the garridge because I've been to look. 'E's not back.'

There was something in his manner, or else I imagined it, which was infuriatingly knowing. It seemed to epitomise the whole of Tinworth's attitude towards me, a sort of pitying condescension, an inquisitive commiseration. It got under my skin.

'I didn't suppose he would be,' I said, and was shocked by something odd in my own tone. I had tried to sound casual and had changed it at the last moment for authority. Williams seemed interested.

'Shall I leave the gates, then?'

I hesitated and he stood waiting.

'What d'ye think?' he enquired at last, and added 'ma'am' as an afterthought.

'Yes, leave them open,' I said. 'It won't do any harm. Good night.'

'Good night, m'm,' I heard him muttering as he bent down to fix the gate-stop. 'Harm?' he was saying. 'Harm?'

The house was dark and quiet as the grave. No one had been in. Everything was just as I had left it. I took Izzy upstairs with me. This was too bad of Victor altogether. I assumed he was punishing me for even daring to try to stand up to him on the evening before. The situation was crazy. I realised it now that I'd faced the problem and slept on it.

Meanwhile Izzy had begun to utter that distinctive Scotty mew which is at once the most apologetic and yet the most demanding sound in the world.

'Well,' I said, 'there's the remains of lunch, chum. We'll go into housekeeping tomorrow when we see what the form is.

Dinner was on the drab side and Izzy enjoyed it more than I did. There was nothing but tepid water out of the bathroom tap to drink, and I discovered that the main boilers from which we were supplied were out and there was no hot water. Finally I had a brain wave and went down to the secretary's room. There I discovered what I expected. Tucked away in a cupboard was a small tin kettle and a half-full packet of tea. There was sugar there and a cup, but no milk, and a gas ring in the fireplace. I made tea.

It was while I was drinking the abominable stuff, and fighting the unreal atmosphere of the empty school buildings crowding in all round me, that it occurred to me that if Victor had been an ordinary normal human being he would at least have left me a message. If he had it would have been a note. He was a man of notes and the whole school seemed to copy him. At Buchanan House no one ever seemed to use a phone or send a verbal message. If they were going to be late for dinner, or the team had won a match, or a leak had been discovered in a bathroom, someone sat down and wrote someone else a little note about it. There was no sign of an envelope upstairs but it occurred to me that he might have left one for me in his study and I went in there to see. There was nothing on the mantelshelf and I went over to the desk and crossed round behind the big chair. There were no loose papers, no miscellany, and certainly no note propped for me to find. Everything was meticulously tidy, as if its owner had cleared up before he left. The only sign of use was the blotter, well inked over because Victor was careful over small matters like stationery and did not have it changed until he had to.

I glanced at it casually and suddenly stood transfixed, my heart jolting on a long and painful beat.

One of my minor accomplishments is that I can read what is called 'mirror writing' quite easily. I had been the overworked editor of a school magazine which had been produced on one of those homemade jelly duplicators, and I had learned the trick to facilitate corrections. Now, as I stood staring at the blotter, a message in Victor's precise handwriting stood out from the rest with startling vividness.

'Thursday the 27th then, my darling. Until . . .
rest assu . . . love you . . . difficult . . . know
that. Always, V.'

I glanced up from the message to the desk
calendar, which was neatly kept to date:
'Thursday, July' and underneath a huge red
'27.'

I ought to have been curious, sick, outraged.
The conventional streak in me which Andy
had pointed out was aware of all the right
reactions, but I felt none of them. I felt freed.

I suppose it was the generations of proud
law-abiding religious women behind me whose
legacies were deep in me, forming my
reactions despite any fancy thinking which I
might be doing on my own account, who
suddenly let up and washed their hands of
Victor. I realised I could go. I was absolved. I
could depart and not look back . . . but not
untidily. That was the last of the iron rules
which must be obeyed. I could go free but I
must not take revenge. I must not ruin him
and above all I must not foul my own nest. He
and I must come to understand one another
and the parting must be arranged without fuss.

I took the sheet of blotting paper out of the
pad and rolled it carefully into a cylinder.

'Come on,' I said to Izzy, 'we can go from here, old boy. But we must tell him first.'

It was about half after midnight, I think, when I decided to try out the home perm outfit on the side pieces of my hair. I had packed most of my clothes and I had very few other possessions because I'd been living rather as if I were in a hotel. Wherever I was going, I shouldn't have much luggage to bother about. I was not sleepy and I was not worried. At last I knew what I had to tell Victor, and I knew I had to do it the moment he came in. I should not look very imposing with my hair in curlers and he'd probably be scandalised by them, but that didn't matter any more. I had plenty of time and I wanted to get it done.

It was quite a business because of the hot water. Izzy and I trotted up and down several times with our kettle, and the directions on the flimsy folder inside the perm packet were long and complicated. All the same, we conquered, and by the time I'd got to *'Operation 8: rinse thoroughly but do not unwind'* the clock on my bedside table said two-fifteen.

I was in the bathroom with my head tied up like a pudding when Izzy began to growl. It was his warning noise, very deep and soft in the back of his throat, and it sent the blood tingling into the nerves of my face and back. I hurried into the bedroom to find him stiff-legged in the middle of the floor, his ears coming off the top of his head, every hair quivering as he faced the open window. Someone was in the courtyard, and since he had not entered presumably it was not Victor. I stood listening and presently I heard an odd splattering sound high up under the window. Izzy growled and started back as a pebble sailed in and rolled on the carpet near him.

I went over at once and put my head out, towel and all.

'What is it?' I demanded.

'Mrs. Lane—?' It was Maureen Jackson's voice and I could just see her in the dusk. She was wrapped in something which I took to be an evening cloak. There was another shadow in the darkness behind her. I could hardly make it out at all and I assumed it was her dancing partner. I drew back at once. My towel was slipping and I was coy about the curlers.

'Yes,' I said from just inside the room, 'what on earth is it?'

'Could—could I possibly speak to the Headmaster?' Her voice was most unnatural and it came to me that she was suppressing giggles. This was most unlike her, of course, but then the hour was not exactly usual. I could hear the engine of a sports car throbbing somewhere in the stillness and I decided that they were on their way home from a party where they had got a little high. Perhaps there had been a lot of gossip about us. Perhaps Victor had been seen with someone. Perhaps

Maureen had been dared to find out if I knew.

'Is he in?'

Something in the question raised a devil in me that I did not know that I possessed. I made a sudden irritable movement and did the silliest thing I have ever done in my life.

'Yes, of course he is,' I said firmly, 'fast asleep, and I shouldn't dream of waking him. Whatever it is must wait till tomorrow. Good night.'

Then I closed the window.

It was a mad thing to do, criminally idiotic. At the time I felt a vague premonition about it, but I did not dream then just how insane it was going to prove to be, for it was not until the following afternoon that Victor's body was discovered and by then he had been dead between twelve and twenty-four hours, so the police doctor said.

PART TWO

The day began quietly enough.

By half past four in the morning I had still had no sleep, although I had been lying on my bed for some time. Izzy was restless too, I noticed, as he lay on the rug before the dressing table. His ears were pricked forward and he whimpered a little every time the school clock struck the quarter hour.

My wretched curlers were abominably uncomfortable and I was tempted to take them out, but I am one of those people who read instructions very carefully and in this case they were specific that five hours was the drying time. I bore the discomfort grimly. *Il faut souffrir être belle,* said the proverb. I didn't know if I was going to look particularly *belle,* but at any rate I thought I'd be a bit better. I had come to hate my role of the forlorn wife, and I was thankful I'd made a start at least to stop looking like one.

At five I got up and made myself another pot of the milkless tea. While I was drinking it, dawn broke and rather guiltily I took another look at the sheet of blotting paper I'd brought upstairs. I wanted to see if I could find out when the revealing message had been written. But all the other fragments were meaningless to me and there seemed nothing to show how long the paper had been in use. I rolled it up again and put it in the long bottom drawer of the chest which I had emptied when I packed.

By this time I had decided where Victor was. I had made up my mind that he had driven to London to meet someone who had probably gone up there from Tinworth by train. I felt fairly certain he had intended to come home during the night but had changed his mind and stayed. I thought he had not telephoned because he had not wanted to bother to make excuses. He knew that I would put up with it, or had decided that it did not matter if I did not.

The more I thought about it the more obvious all this appeared. The tone of the note had suggested an old love affair, which argued that the woman, whoever she was, probably was one of the local ladies who had caused the scandal last winter. It was because of that scandal that I thought they wouldn't risk spending an evening together nearer than the city, and I guessed he had not kept me informed because he knew that I would never fly into a panic and start telephoning round the town. He had trained me never to do that. There had been a most unfortunate incident a few weeks after our marriage when Victor had gone over to Tortham College for an evening conference. The meeting had gone on much longer than anyone had expected and he had accepted a bed from one of the housemasters without letting me know. I had got frightened that he might have had an accident with the car and had telephoned the Head's house at one in the morning. My call had caused no end of fuss in that fortress of academic conventionalism, and the savagery and the sarcasm of the reprimand I had received from Victor still brought the colour to my face whenever I remembered it. It had not been very fair, of course, but then that had been one of the lessons which had taught me not to expect ordinary fair behaviour from the man I had married.

I crawled back into my bed and lay there wondering who the woman was. I was ashamed of myself for not feeling more bitter about her. All my upbringing had taught that a good wife ought to know by some sort of magical divination the woman whom her husband prefers, but my intelligence warned me that this was moonshine. Victor had always kept me at arm's length. I did not know him. I did not know his taste, even.

I thought I had only closed my eyes for an instant, but when I opened them again the sun was pouring in through the window, Izzy was barking like a lunatic, and standing at the end of my bed was a little old woman in a bright overall and a shabby black hat which boasted a bunch of tousled but valiant feathers in it. She was watching me with a strange intensity, her eyes very wide open and her thin nose twitching like Izzy's own.

' 'E's gorn,' she said with dramatic

suddenness. ' 'Is bed ain't slep' in. Did you know?'

I lay looking at her stupidly for a moment while all the facts slowly reassembled themselves in my mind, and I remembered the charwoman Miss Richardson had promised to send me.

'You're Mrs. Veal,' I said at last.

'That's right.' Her unnerving gaze never left my face. 'Come to do for yer. 'Aven't slep', 'ave yer?'

'Not very well,' I admitted, struggling up into a sitting position and wondering what on earth had happened to my head that I should feel as if it had been scalped. 'What's the time? Nine?' I stared at the clock on the bedside table with unfocusing eyes. 'How awful. I'm so sorry.'

'Don't you move.' In Mrs. Veal's dramatic tones, which I had not yet learned were habitual with her, the words were a command. 'Stay where you are. You 'aven't slep' a wink, you 'aven't. I saw it as soon as I come in. Lie there until I get you a cuppertea, and particularly don't look at yerself in the glass. It'll give yer a turn. You look like a pore young corp. Don't you worry about nothing. I've got milk in me bag *and* a small brown loaf. "There won't be nothing there," Miss Richardson said, and so I come prepared.' She paused for breath and gave me another searching stare. 'You *can't* 'ave slep'. I saw my sister's youngest when the undertaker had done with 'er and she looked more alive than you do now, and that's the truth. Tossin' and turnin' all night, that's what you must 'ave been. Lie where you are until I come back.'

She scuttled out as suddenly as she had arrived and I pulled myself wearily out of bed and peered fearfully in the looking glass. The sight was almost reassuring. It was still me. I looked a bit of a mess and my eyes were smudgy and hollow, but I was recognisable. I began to pull out the curlers which had made my head ache, and was gratified to see a gentle but unmistakable wave. I put a comb through it gingerly, but it persisted and there was no sign of the frizzing I had feared. I was still examinining my handiwork when the door opened unceremoniously.

'There's no kitchen in this 'ouse.' Sheer astonishment seemed to have robbed Mrs. Veal of her histrionic powers. She spoke almost mildly.

'No,' I said, and added almost idiotically, 'I know.'

'No kitchen!'

'Well,' I began apologetically, 'you see, in the ordinary way the school . . .'

'Oh yers, I daresay.' She swept my explanation aside with magnificent contempt. 'The school looks after yer like a mother, I don't doubt, but *no kitchen* . . . and they call it a gentleman's residence. Well, I never did, I *never* did! I didn't really. I'll go straight to Mrs. Williams and see what she can provide and no one shall stop me.'

She was gone again with the speed of a bird, only to put her head in a moment later.

'No master in 'is bed and no kitchen,' she remarked devastatingly. 'Whatever next?'

She went out again and I hurried after her and called to her down the stairs. It had occurred to me that if she was going into the Williamses I ought to make some sort of excuse for Victor's absence, since I'd asked the porter to leave the gate for him.

'It'll only be breakfast for one, Mrs. Veal,' I said, 'and I shan't want anything much. The Headmaster rang up late last night. He's been detained in London.'

She paused without looking round. I could see her little figure foreshortened on the stairs below me. Presently she turned and peered up.

'What yer going to do for 'is dinner?'

'What? Oh, I'll think of something. We'll probably go into the town. I don't know when he's coming home, you see. I expect he'll ring again.'

'I see.' She sounded very dubious. 'Don't know when 'e's coming.' She nodded as if it was a lesson she had learned and I suddenly realised that she must have had a word or so with the Williamses already. I went back to my bedroom and began to dress. I felt trapped again, back in the atmosphere of gossip and commiseration. I was very conscious of being a bad liar, too, and I was furious with Victor for putting me in a position where these white lies seemed so necessary.

I was in the little dining room when Mrs. Veal returned. She came steaming up the stairs with a laden tray which she placed proudly on the table before me.

'She done the lot, Mrs. Williams did. Wouldn't even look at me brown loaf. Said she was only too pleased,' she announced breathlessly as she prepared to whip off the white napkin with which the offering was covered. 'She's a real good woman, a real good woman, in spite of 'er being under the doctor with 'er legs. Nothink is too much trouble. Is it yer birthday?'

The sudden question bewildered me. 'Birthday?'

'Yes, well, as I said, you never said nothink to me about it, but we wondered if it was yer birthday because of the present, you see.' She removed the covering and displayed a pyramid of stiff white florist's paper amid the breakfast things. 'The doctor brought it' she rattled on, 'the young one with the eyes. You know. 'E's doing the job while the old gentleman, 'oo is a bit past it, is on 'is 'olidays. He never took an 'oliday before 'e was on the Government, so it shows yer, don't it?'

I laughed. She was doing me good. She was what I needed, a human voice. It occurred to

69

me that if I'd met her before my ignorance of the real and inner life of Tinworth would not be nearly so abysmal. All the same I was shaken by the flowers. It wasn't like Andy to do anything so graceful. I took off the wrappings and smiled. It was a little clump of speckled blue flowers in a small ornamental bowl. I'd seen some like it in the good florist's next the cinema. It was a line they were selling that month and it looked like Andy, charming and unpretentious and somehow solid. The envelope which the florist provided to hold the card was stuck down and I tore it open unsuspecting. The message was scribbled in the handwriting I had once known so very well.

Clearing out today. Fixed it with the local man. All the best, Andy.

I sat staring at it until I became aware that the colour was pouring up my neck and into my face. It was dismay, and yet I had not once permitted myself to hope that our good-byes had not been final. How strange it was, I thought suddenly, that one's body seems to go on living a life of its own, feeling emotions and reacting to them however strictly one makes one's mind behave.

I glanced up to find Mrs. Veal watching me with unveiled curiosity. There was nothing of the ghoul about her. She was perfectly friendly and quite clearly on my side, but she liked to know what was going on.

'It suits yer, that bit o' colour in yer face,' she remarked disconcertingly. 'Now you've got it you look better-looking, more like you did when you first come. It's the bit of a curl, I suppose. It's wonderful what it does for yer. That young doctor's goin' away.'

'Oh, is he?' I said in an ineffectual attempt to sound casual.

'So Mrs. Williams told me. She's ever so sorry. 'E come round early to take a last look at 'er legs. Nice of 'im, wasn't it? Some wouldn't, that they wouldn't, not today. 'E said 'e was off. Couldn't stick it, 'e said. Known 'im long, 'ave yer?'

It was one of those direct questions which cannot be sidetracked, so I said we were both on the same hospital staff before I was married.

'Oh, I see.' It was obvious that she did, too, the whole story. I could see it in the wisdom of her old grey eyes. 'Oh well,' she said, giving me a friendly little grimace, 'It's just as well, ain't it? I mean people are always ready to talk in a place like this. You mayn't believe it but you'd be surprised. It's not like London. Make up anything, they will, *and* say it. So it's just as well 'e's gorn. Per'aps 'e saw it 'isself. Nice of 'im to send the flowers, wasn't it? I'll put 'em on the side. There, don't they look pretty?'

'Very,' I agreed faintly. 'I—er, I don't know what they are, do you?'

'Nemo-phila,' said the amazing woman calmly. 'They grow a lot of 'em round 'ere, for seed. They mean *"may success crown your wishes."* That's surprised yer, ain't it?'

'It staggers me.'

She laughed. 'I used to work in a card factory when I was a girl. Birthday cards we used to make, very elaborate. We were give the cards, see, with the motters and a pictcher on 'em, and then we 'ad to stick on the right pressed flower. There was lots of 'em. *"Thoughts I bring you"*—that was pansies, and oh, I don't know what else. Come on, drink yer coffee. So there you are, *"success crown your wishes,"* that's what 'e sent you.' She hesitated, honesty getting the better of her romanticism. 'I don't really suppose 'e knew.'

'Perhaps not.'

'Still it was very nice of 'im. You'll remember 'im gratefully.'

I thought she was going to leave me at last but she still hovered.

'Oh, and there's this,' she said, planking a crumpled piece of paper on the cloth before me. 'Williams give me this to bring over. If the master wasn't 'ere, 'e said, perhaps you'd look after it. It's the receipt for the luggage, see?'

'The . . .?' I checked my exclamation and took up the paper. It was not easy to decipher. My hand seemed to be shaking so much that I could hardly see it. Mrs. Veal explained. Her fund of information seemed to be inexhaustible.

'It's the master's climbing-luggage, the 'eavy stuff that's kep' in the locker room. It's gorn to Switzerland to be ready for 'im. It's sent every year. Williams always sees to it. 'E told Williams to get it off for 'im and Williams did, yesterday.'

'When was Williams told?' For the life of me I could not keep the revealing sharpness out of my voice.

'Oh, I don't know, dear, I mean madam. Sometime in the term, I expec'. Didn't the master tell yer?'

'I expect he forgot.'

'Yes, well, they are forgetful, aren't they, men are. Can't 'elp themselves. So bloomin' conceited they don't know if they're goin' or comin' 'alf the time. Still, it'll be a weight off your mind, won't it, to know it's safely sent? You're goin' with 'im this time, are yer? When you settin' off?'

'Soon. I'm not quite sure, exactly.'

She clicked her tongue against her teeth with tolerant commiseration. 'Keep us on the 'op, don't they, all the time? Well, I'll get on.' She went out at last and left me with the receipt. I folded it carefully and tucked it into the little Chinese vase on the mantelshelf. The whole incident had alarmed me. If Victor had made this arrangement without telling me, what others might he have fixed? For one wild moment it went through my mind he might have just gone off on his trip already, calling in somewhere on the way to see the lady of the note. Perhaps I should get a letter sometime during the day telling me what he'd decided and enclosing a little money for me to carry on with. It seemed incredible, but only because I envisaged it happening to *me*. I had heard of husbands who behaved like that, and what was worse, I knew that if I simply related the fact to some disinterested person—a lawyer for instance—it was by no means certain that he would be sympathetic. How was he to know that it was not merely some phase in a private sex war between us? There would be only my word for it. At that moment I could see, as never before, that the way Victor treated me was my business, and the only person on earth who could do anything about it was myself.

If Victor had behaved like this I'd have to go after him. I went into his room and tried to discover which of his clothes were missing. A more experienced wife would have thought of this before, of course, but once again I was at a disadvantage. Victor's personal affairs had been under control for years before I had appeared on the scene. There was a sort of resident batman, a school valet, who had made it part of his work to look after Victor's clothes and to attend to his mending and laundry, so I had never been permitted to interfere. The man came in every so often, and must now have gone off on holiday with everyone else. I went through the wardrobe and chest, but apart from the fact that I recognised some of the items they might have belonged to a stranger. I simply couldn't tell if a modest holiday outfit had been packed and taken away. The bed was made up with clean sheets and there were no soiled pajamas about, but on the other hand there seemed a good stock of clean pairs in the drawer. The bathroom was more revealing. His shaving things were there in the toilet cupboard. I realised he might well possess a small travelling outfit, but I had never seen one and I felt mildly comforted. I thought perhaps after all he intended to come back and explain before going abroad. He wasn't going to behave quite so disgustingly. All the same, it was not conclusive evidence, by any means, and after a while I got nervy again and went down to his study.

It was just as I'd last seen it, very bare and shiny. The clean sheet of blotting paper in the folder on the desk made the gleaming expanse of mahogany look even more deserted. I opened the drawers tentatively. They were all very tidy, papers pinned neatly together, letters in spring clips, folders tidily stacked. The school servants were very good, I reflected idly. The polish on every wooden surface was perfect. My finger marks seemed to show wherever I put them. I'd have rubbed them off after me but I hadn't a duster, and I recollected that the place was to be left for a couple of months.

Here again, as in the bedroom, I could tell so little because I knew so little. We never sat in the study and there were very few occasions when I had even entered it. It was Victor's workroom. I had only seen the desk drawers open half a dozen times. I did not go through the papers; I could not bear to. The notion of finding a bundle of incriminating letters from some wretched local girl filled me with such distaste that I was astonished at myself, and I suddenly realised how lucky I was. I realised some women must find themselves in just this same position but with one vital difference. If I had ever loved Victor, then I should have tasted bitterness. As it was, I was hurt and even outraged, and what pride I had was suffering badly, but I was not annihilated. It was my ideals and beliefs and conventions which were crushed, but not the basic me. He had not touched that because it had never belonged to him. And then I thought that if I'd loved him this would never have happened quite like this. I'd have known more about him. We were both to blame. A marriage without love is not marriage. We were playing at it, Victor and I. We were not married at all and it had taken me six months to find out.

I closed the last drawer and stood back. There was only one thing missing that I remembered seeing there before and that was a revolver. It was a big army thing in a service holster. It had lain in the back of the middle drawer and I had seen it there one day in the winter when I had taken Victor some typing he had asked me to do for him. He had opened the drawer to get a clip for the sheets and I had seen the gun and commented on it. He told me that he kept it as a souvenir of the war, and that he had a licence for it, and I said that with so many children about it was dangerous and that he ought to keep it in the safe. Now that it had gone I assumed that he had agreed with me, and I was glad to have had some little influence over him, however small.

I looked round the room again but there was nothing left about, not even a newspaper. The only thing in the least untidy was the charred sheet in the empty grate, a single oblong, quite large. I only noticed it idly and I had no time to consider it or the odd little incident which had put it there, for just then the telephone bell sounded from the deserted secretary's room just across the hall. I caught my breath. This was it. Now I should hear some sort of explanation and I knew I must take myself in hand and be as firm and as ruthless as he.

But when I took up the receiver it was not Victor but a much slower, deeper voice which greeted me. I must have been in hypersensitive mood that morning, for although it was the first time that ever I heard it, yet it made me vaguely uneasy from the start. I can only say it sounded friendly but sly, like an uncle asking trick questions.

'Would that be Buchanan House? I wonder if I could speak to the Headmaster, Mr. Lane. It's the police here as a matter of fact. Superintendent South. Just put me through to him, will you?'

'I'm sorry,' I said, 'he's out.'

'Oh. And when are you expecting him back?'

'I'm afraid I don't know.'

'I see.' The avuncular voice sounded dubious. 'Would that be Mrs. Lane by any chance?'

'Yes. Can I help you?'

'Well, I don't know, Mrs. Lane. It's a little difficult. It's an enquiry from the Metropolitan Police, Northern Division, about a John O'Farrell Rorke.'

'Pardon? What's happened to him?'

'Well, he seems to have been involved in an accident and quite a nasty one. He's in the Watling Street Hospital with multiple injuries, but he seems to have been inebriated at the time and the driver of the bus which ran him down has got a story which has got to be confirmed. Meanwhile, the police want details of any relatives he may have. He's unconscious and the only address they have is the school's. They got that from a couple of envelopes in his pocket.'

'I'm terribly sorry, and I don't see how I can help,' I began. 'I don't know anything about Mr. Rorke's home life, but I'll tell my husband to ring you the moment he comes in. Meanwhile, I wonder if you'd like to ring his secretary? She might know something.'

There was silence for a moment and then he said, 'Would that be Miss Maureen Jackson?'

'Yes. She knows . . .'

He cut me short. 'As a matter of fact, Mrs. Lane, I've been on to her already. I know her quite well, d'you see? She and her family are old friends of mine. I thought of her at once and I rang her because I wasn't sure if the Headmaster had gone off on his holiday or not, and I thought it would save time.' He laughed apologetically, but making it quite clear to me that he was as parochial and gossipy as anyone else in the town. He added shamelessly, 'We have to save time, you know, Mrs. Lane. Maureen, that is, Miss Jackson— she's in bed with a chill, by the way—told me that Mr. Lane was at home last night so I thought I'd catch him.'

I hesitated. I nearly told him that I hadn't seen Victor for twenty-four hours and that I'd lied to Maureen because she had irritated me. It would have been an embarrassing confession but I have an ingrained respect for the police and I am fairly certain I would have done it if I hadn't realised that he was on neighbourly terms with the Jacksons and guessed the sort of chatter which must inevitably have followed. As it was, I simply said good-bye.

'I'll tell him to ring you as soon as he comes in,' I finished.

He was not satisfied. 'Do you know where he's gone, Mrs. Lane? I'd like to get hold of him.'

'No, I'm afraid I don't.'

'Did he take his car?'

'Yes.'

'And he didn't leave any message, didn't say anything at all? Just drove away?'

'No.' It was beginning to sound awful and I groped round for something to say which would at least convey that we were more or less on speaking terms. The Superintendent forestalled me.

'He'll be in for lunch anyway, won't he?'

'I don't know. I mean, the school is shut. We're not eating here. I think he will be back this morning, but I—I . . .' I made a great effort to struggle out of the morass of words and succeeded. 'I know,' I said suddenly, 'I know who is sure to be able to help you. Do you know Mr. Seckker?'

'Now that's an idea, Mrs. Lane.' To my relief the Superintendent gave up worrying about Victor at once. He sounded approving. 'Mr. Seckker's a—friend of Mr. Rorke's, is he?'

'I think so, in a way.'

There was a laugh at the other end of the wire. 'You're going to say that Mr. Seckker is a friend of every lame duck.' The voice had lost its slyness and sounded merely hearty. 'You're right there. So he is. I'll get on to him immediately. But, Mrs. Lane, do tell your husband the moment he comes in, because I think there may be a bit of trouble about this case—or not trouble, exactly, but publicity, and a thing like that never does a school any good. A word from your husband now might save a lot of bother later on. See what I mean?'

'I do,' I assured him. 'Thank you very much.'

'Not at all. We're all very proud of the school in Tinworth, so it's in everybody's interest to keep everything clean and sweet. So if you do happen to remember where your husband's gone this morning, and you can reach him on the telephone, have a try, see? Good morning.'

'Good morning,' I said huskily, and hung up.

I made a note on a pad for Victor and left the sheet propped up on the hall table where he could not fail to see it. Then I went slowly upstairs.

I told Mrs. Veal that Mr. Rorke had been run over. There seemed no harm in telling her and it kept her from chattering about Victor or, what was worse still, Andy. She had put the bowl of flowers in the middle of the dining-room table, I saw, and was prepared to mention it as soon as I appeared. My news sidetracked her.

'Run over? In hospital?' She echoed my words with genuine pity. 'What a shame! What a shame after all 'e's done to keep 'imself you-know-what after all this time. Never once, never once not in two terms 'as 'e been—well, we-won't-mention-it. I was only saying so to Mr. Williams. "It's a miracle," I said, "and 'e ought to 'ave a medal for it." It's not easy, no, it's not easy, that it isn't, to keep yerself you-know-what once you've let it get 'old of you like 'e did. And now runned over as well. I never!'

She made herself perfectly plain for all her ladylike censorship and I understood why Mr. Rorke had not struck me as the drinker his reputation had suggested. His sobriety since I had met him had been the result of effort. I had not realised that.

'I am afraid the end of term was too much for him,' I murmured.

She considered me with serious eyes and nodded her head like a Chinese mandarin.

'The night before last, that was when it started again. Pore chap! As I said to Williams, you would 'ave thought 'e'd 'ave waited until 'e got off school premises, I said, but no, 'e couldn't. Down the town 'e went and come back when the pubs closed, swearing. Williams

82

says—well, 'e couldn't tell me what 'e said and I'm sure I didn't want to 'ear.

'It's a great pity,' I said. 'I had not realised it was a habit with him.'

'It used not to be,' she assured me earnestly. 'Not for years, it wasn't. And then last year it seemed to come over 'im and it was quite bad. Then there was the noise at the end of the winter term and we all thought 'e'd pulled 'isself together.'

'Noise?' I enquired, fascinated.

She dropped her eyes modestly. 'Some persons say "row,"' she explained primly, 'but it's not a very nice expression. 'E did somethink and the 'Eadmaster 'eard of it and oh my! We all thought 'e'd 'ave to leave, we did really. Then it all flowed over and the next term—that was the term you come—'e was as good as gold and sober as a judge. Did 'im good.'

I felt I ought not to gossip but she seemed to hold the key to the school and to Tinworth. No one else had been half so informative. In fact she was the only person who had treated me like a woman. Everyone else had seemed to think I was a new boy.

'What did he do?' I enquired guiltily.

'I'm not dead certain.' She lowered her voice conspiratorially. 'But we understood at the time that 'e said something to one of the boys—I'm not sure 'e didn't write it, which would 'ave been worse—something in the swearing line, it was. The boy was a bit soft and told 'is parents, and the parents was a bit soft and told the 'Eadmaster. That's what we 'eard. There *was* a to-do! The 'Ead, well, 'e can use 'is tongue, can't 'e? Sarcastic? Vinegar's milk when 'e gets goin', vinegar's milk, I say.'

She glanced at me anxiously. 'Not that I ought to say such a thing to you, dear—I mean madam. I must get on. Still I'm sorry that Mr. Rorke's runned over, I am indeed. People are never the same again after that 'appens, sober or—well, we won't mention it. No, they're *not*.'

She began to sweep with great vigour and since there was nothing I could do I took Izzy and we went round the school grounds, battered and deserted in the morning sun. I saw no one at all. No one was at work. No one came up the drive. No tradesmen. No visitor. No boy.

I sat down on one of the well-worn seats on which generations of children had carved their names, and waited, watching the gates, but there was no sign of Victor. Finally I saw Mrs. Veal wobble off down the path on a bone-shaking bicycle. She waved to me and shouted that she'd 'see me termorrer' and then she was gone and I was quite alone. I thought of Rorke and wished there was something I could have done for him. He seemed to be an unhappy sort of person, probably most unsuited to be a schoolmaster, and yet someone had said that he taught brilliantly. Possibly it had been Victor; I couldn't remember. At any rate, I was glad that Mr. Seckker would be his rescuer on behalf of the school. I felt pretty certain that if one was in some sort of scrape it would be nicer to be rescued by Mr. Seckker than by Victor.

My thoughts returned to Victor and I rehearsed what I had decided I must say to him. I could imagine his opening sarcasms as he began to reply, but I had made up my mind that I must wear all that down. I must stand up to it and defeat it and get my point into his head. Andy was always creeping back into my mind but I pushed him out resolutely. As Mrs. Veal had put it so devastatingly, it was just as well he'd gone, and perhaps he'd seen it himself.

At last I went back to the house, dressed myself for the street with as much care as possible, and, taking Izzy on a lead, went down the town. Izzy loathed the lead but he was a fighter, and I seldom dared to take him into a crowd where every second woman had a dog with her. However, today I did not feel like parting with him even for a moment.

The Flower Club lecture was at a quarter after two in the Public Library's smaller room, and I thought I'd go. It seemed to me that I'd found out a great deal about Tinworth in the last twenty-four hours, and I wanted to see all these people who had seemed so unaccountably alien to me during the few months I had known them, in the light of all this new information. It was a chance I did not imagine I should have again. Everyone would be there. The Flower Club was Tinworth's latest craze. It was amusing, it was elegant, and it was cheap.

As in most British provincial towns, even the well-to-do ladies of Tinworth managed their lives on a very rigid budget and local crafts and crazes were apt to fade very quickly if the materials required cost even a little actual money spent. Flowers had the enormous advantage of being practically free. Everybody grew flowers; the seed fields round the town were full of them and the gardens bloomed like the Sunday hats of long ago. So the art of floral decoration flourished, and the cult took on a seriousness which was almost Japanese. In that year the Flower Club was definitely the thing to join, so I should have plenty of opportunity of seeing everyone. As I walked down the road I reflected that I must also eat. This idiotic business of my being taken so utterly by surprise by the sudden closing down of the school commissariat had shaken me more than I cared to admit. I am not incapable. I was quite able to cater and care for myself and a family, and I was eager to do it. To be caught out like this suddenly, without even a saucepan or a stove to put it on and no way of telling what, if anything, was required of me, put me in wrong. I did not like to rush out and buy some temporary equipment which I should not need for long, because I had very little money. This was another irritation. I was used to earning a reasonable living, but I had no inheritance and after six months my savings were dwindling rapidly.

I bought myself a cheap lunch at the Olde Worlde Teashoppe in the High Street and managed to smuggle half of it to Izzy, hidden behind me on the olde worlde settle. We dawdled over it as long as we decently could and then went over to the Library.

The staircase was cool and quiet after the sun-baked streets and I assumed I was the first to arrive, but as I crossed the landing I saw that the doors of the lecture room were open and heard the sibilant mutter of voices inside. I picked up Izzy and, carrying him under my arm, walked in.

As I appeared on the threshold there was sudden and absolute silence.

The big shabby room was dim as a church and nearly as cool, with the same smell of dust and paper faint in the air. The rows of cane chairs stretching up towards the platform made a vast flimsy barrier between me and the four women who stood together in the aisle before the front row. For a full minute they stood quite still, a picture of arrested movement, their bodies still bent towards each other as if they had been whispering. But every head was turned, every face blank, every eye watching me. It only lasted a short time but it was long enough to tell me that they had been discussing me.

I did not care in the least. At last I felt sure once again that I knew a great deal more about my own business than anyone else did, and that was a very good feeling.

I knew all four women slightly. There was the inevitable Mrs. Raye, looking at least half ashamed of herself; Mrs. Roundell, the pretty, pleasant wife of the Town Clerk; Miss Bonwitt, a slightly vague spinster who was chiefly remarkable for her wonderful garden out on the hill above the golf course; and Mrs. Amy Petty.

Amy Petty was rather better known to me than the others. She was Maureen Jackson's widowed elder sister, for one thing, and I had met her calling at the school several times. She had the Jackson family's direct manner, their money and their clannishness, but her face was like a mean little hen's set atop a long flat figure clad in very good but very ugly country clothes.

I had often thought that for some reason she disliked me, but in the normal way she was polite enough. Today she astonished me by letting her eyes flicker away from me without a gleam of recognition, while her mouth shut in a firm hard button. It was a brief reaction, and by the time I had found my way round the chairs towards her she was pleasant, yet there was something new and strange about her which I did not understand. The idea seemed ridiculous, but it did go through my mind that she was behaving as if she were afraid of me.

There was something strange about them all. Even Mrs. Raye did not seem sure of herself. It struck me as odd at the time because Tinworth ladies were so often caught gossiping by the subjects of their scandal that it was hardly considered a social contretemps any longer. The conversation began jerkily, with me the only person quite at ease.

Mrs. Raye said it was good of me to come. Miss Bonwitt agreed with her rather too quickly. Mrs. Roundell hoped the lecturer wasn't going to make flower arrangement too scientific, and Amy Petty asked me bluntly if I knew when I was going on my holiday. I was prepared for that one by this time and I said the day was not actually fixed but I expected to be off by the end of the week. Hester Raye came back into form at that point and slid her arm through mine.

'My dear,' she said, her words tumbling over one another in her usual rush, 'the Chief Constable and I were wondering if you and your husband could come to dinner with us tomorrow night? I do know it's terribly short notice and I am so sorry, but we've been terribly rushed lately and I do want to fit you in.'

I opened my mouth but she forestalled me.

'Don't say no until you've heard me. We've got some quite interesting people coming—the Wedgwoods, the Rippers, that girl Sally French, and—oh, by the way, did you know that that nice young doctor of yours had gone? Left the town, my dear. Fixed it up with young Pettigrew, wrote Dr. Browning, and simply left. I believe it was fearfully sudden. He made up his mind last night. Dick Pettigrew told me.' Her eyes peered brightly into mine. 'Perhaps you knew about it?'

'I—I wasn't surprised. I mean it doesn't astonish me.' It was not a good effort on my part but then she had flustered me, as she always did with her well-meaning blunderbuss tactics.

'You'd known him before, had you, Mrs. Lane? I thought he was a complete stranger.' This came from little Mrs. Roundell, trying to be nice in her fluttering ingenuous way. 'We all liked him so much. He attended Mother last week and she adored him. Said he was sweet.'

'And now he's gone.' Hester Raye grimaced. 'Just our luck in Tinworth. Well now, Mrs. Lane, what about tomorrow? Could you pin Victor down for a quarter to eight or eight o'clock? Do come.' She was still holding my arm and now she shook it slightly and came out with one of her typical pronouncements. 'My Reggie is dying to see you both. I told him all about meeting you yesterday and he was terribly intrigued. He's been worried about you too, you know, just as we all have.'

How she dared say it! She took my breath away, although she had long since ceased to amaze me. I could not believe that the old Chief Constable, who was a very decent but not particularly sensitive man, could have grieved much on my account, but I could easily guess what she had told him.

It was on the tip of my tongue to say that I did not imagine that Victor and I would ever be going out to dinner together again, but that after all was a thing that Victor had a right to know before anybody else and so I merely stalled.

'It's very kind of you,' I said, 'but I really think you'll have to count us out. I don't think I dare fix up anything definite at the moment.'

'Why ... not?' This was Amy Petty. She spoke too sharply and too brashly for even the known Jackson family manner to excuse her. Everybody turned and stared at her. She looked very odd, her small eyes defiant and bright spots of colour on her high cheekbones. She said no more but stood her ground, waiting for me to reply. In the end I had to say something.

'I'm not at all sure what Victor has fixed,' I explained. 'He's in London at the moment and I'm not quite sure when he'll be back.'

It seemed an ordinary social

pronouncement to me but its effect was extraordinary. There was dead silence. Amy Petty remained looking at me while everybody else glanced awkwardly away.

'He was home last night. You told my sister so.' The words were forced out of Amy. She was being more impolite than even Tinworth permitted and she realised it, but she appeared to be incapable of controlling herself. I felt almost sorry for her.

'Why yes,' I said glibly, more, I think, with the idea of putting her at ease than for any other reason, 'so I did. I thought I'd heard him come in, you see, but he was detained in London and couldn't get back. He telephoned this morning.'

There was a little sigh from them all. Mrs. Roundell alone smiled contentedly, as though to say that she had been right after all, and I was just going to pass on down the row to find myself a seat when Miss Bonwitt, who until now had been perfectly silent, said quietly: 'I am so glad. It was his car, you see. There is just one place in my garden where one can look down through the trees and see it in that corner by the cottage wall.' She had one of those high-pitched apologetic voices which seemed to make every pronouncement sound like a spirit message, inconclusive but faintly ominous.

I swung round on her, startled into frankness. 'Cottage?' I demanded.

'Yes, your cottage. Mr. Lane's little cottage,' she continued placidly. 'I daresay you feel it's quite remote out there on the edge of the golf course. I know if it were mine, I should. But actually, as I say, there is one point in my garden where one can look round the shoulder of the hill and see down through the leaves right into the corner where Mr. Lane parks his car. I can't see any other part of the cottage, just that one wall at the back. I happened to notice the car there yesterday and naturally I thought nothing of it, but when I went to the same place this morning to see if I'd dropped one of my gardening gloves I saw the car was still in the same place.'

I stood staring at her, my face drawn and frozen. The cottage! I thought. Oh, how *could* Victor do such a thing so near, so dangerously near? How *could* he subject himself and me to this humiliation?

'Go and look for him, Mrs. Lane.' Once again Amy Petty spoke explosively, as if she could not keep the words back.

'Oh no,' I protested far too violently, 'no, of course not. I mean to say, I think Miss Bonwitt must have caught sight of the car on the only two occasions when it happened to be there. I know Victor was calling at the cottage to—to take some things on his way to town, and I expect he called there on the way back. He keeps his golf clubs there, of course. He's probably home by now.'

Miss Bonwitt shook her wispy grey head at me and I noticed for the first time that her eyes were hooded, with webby lids, and were not just dull as I had always thought.

'Oh no,' she said in a quiet singsong, 'it wasn't like that, Mrs. Lane, it wasn't like that at all. I first noticed the car about four o'clock yesterday afternoon when I was tying up my chrysanthemums, and when I went in about seven it was still there. This morning I got up very early because there is a lot to do in the garden, and it is so cool and pleasant in the dawn. I was out about five and, as I say, I went up to the chrysanthemums to see if I had dropped one of my gloves. The car was still there with the hood still down and the rug half hanging out as I'd seen it before. I did wonder, because you know we had a very sharp shower during the night.'

'Victor must have forgotten it,' I murmured, and even to my own ears I sounded idiotic.

'I hope so,' murmured Miss Bonwitt, 'I hope so indeed. But since the car was still there, and still in exactly the same condition when I set out for the lecture three quarters of an hour ago, I did wonder if Mr. Lane could have been taken ill up there alone. I was just mentioning it to the others when you came in . . . Mrs. Lane.'

She made it sound frightful. Although her voice was placid and there were no undertones in it, yet she made it perfectly clear to everybody that she had watched the car all through the hours during which there was light enough to see it.

Hester Raye attempted to come to my rescue in a pleasant heavy way. She had her faults and was often rude, but she had the remnants of a decent upbringing and Amy Petty's performance had shocked her.

'But if Mrs. Lane says Victor telephoned this morning there's some other explanation for the car,' she said cheerfully. 'Quite probably someone gave him a lift to London from the golf club so he hid his own car. It sounds as if it was hidden if it was in such a funny place, behind the cottage, I mean, and not in front.'

'Yes,' said Miss Bonwitt quietly, 'no one could have seen it from the road. That's why I wondered.'

She was silent for a long time and I felt myself shudder. It was a rather extraordinary and unlikely thing for Victor to do. I could believe he might be sufficiently inconsiderate to entertain someone at the cottage for an hour or so, even, since he seemed to have made an effort to conceal the car, all the evening, but I couldn't think that he'd stay there all day, especially without looking at his car. He was fussy about things like that. I had not noticed that there had been a shower, but Victor would have made sure, particularly if he had left the hood down.

'I suppose he did telephone, Mrs. Lane?' continued Miss Bonwitt after her long pause, and she raised her wrinkled lids and gave me a surprisingly intelligent stare. 'Himself, I mean?' She was offering me an easy way out and I hesitated. It occurred to me that she knew rather a lot and had probably seen things before when she was tying up flowers at seven at night or pottering about in the dawn. I did not know what to say. It was rather peculiar, rather alarming.

'Who sent the message, my dear?' Hester Raye's practical mind was troubled. 'Who spoke on the telephone?'

'It came from his club,' I said. It was the only lie I could think of and I hated it and myself and wished to goodness I'd stuck to the truth in the first place. If Victor *had* been taken ill, broken an ankle or something, as they suggested, I had put up some fine behaviour!

Little Mrs. Roundell laughed and clapped her hands. 'How mysterious!' she said. 'Or didn't you get it right? I often don't. I hate telephones. Percival says I'm mentally defective when it comes to messages. People gabble and the thing goes plop-plop-squeak, and you get cut off . . .'

'Go out there and see, Mrs. Lane. I'll drive you.' Amy Petty made it a command and when I glanced at her I saw that there was a queer sick look in her small eyes.

Hester Raye objected. 'Not *now*,' she said with characteristic blindness to everything but her own convenience. 'Not before the lecture. The hall is filling up, thank God, but there aren't nearly enough people here yet. My lecturer will be here any minute. Stay. You must stay for the talk.'

'But if he has been taken *ill*,' said Miss Bonwitt with gentle firmness, 'and I think he has, you know—the car has never been there so long bef . . . I mean I think she ought to make sure. Mrs. Raye, I do indeed. I think Mrs. Lane really ought to make sure.'

Amy Petty's big thin hand closed over my shoulder blade as if she were arresting me, and Izzy, feeling me jump, growled at her from my arms.

'Go and see.'

'I would,' announced Mrs. Roundell with sudden decision. 'I think I would. Telephones are the limit, and if he's there in pain or something, well, you'd never forgive yourself, would you? Just go and make sure and then tear back. I'll bag some seats for you near the door. Then you can just slip in.'

'I'll never forgive you two if you clear off now,' Mrs. Raye began, but turned away with a cry of welcome as a stout woman with her arms full of mixed flowers, followed by a pale girl staggering under a tray of vases, came sweeping down the hall towards us.

Amy Petty turned me bodily towards the

nearest exit. 'I'll drive you,' she repeated woodenly.

I went out into the side street which runs down past the back door of the Library with her, but as I reached the pavement I hesitated.

'Don't trouble,' I said. 'I'll go back and get a bicycle. You go to the lecture.'

'No. I'll come with you. My brother will drive us.'

I stared at her. I knew she had eight or nine brothers, in fact Tinworth appeared to be populated with Jackson menfolk, but I hardly expected to find one standing about in the street waiting to do taxi work.

'Good heavens, no!' I exclaimed so loudly that a woman passing turned to look at us. I recognised her as the younger of the two sisters who kept the Teashoppe. I smiled at her awkwardly. 'You certainly won't,' I added to Amy. 'It's probably all nonsense. I'll go home and see if Victor's back and if he isn't I'll cycle over to the cottage and investigate.'

'No. We'll drive you.' The Jacksons seemed to be obstinate as well as outspoken. 'Come along.'

I went with her, her determination adding to my growing alarm. I was through with Victor and in the moments when I permitted myself to think about him, I rather hated him, but I didn't like the idea of him lying helpless on a stone floor with a broken leg, him or anybody else. After Miss Bonwitt's tale about the car I knew I'd got to go to the cottage.

As we came over the road I realised why Amy had mentioned her brother. Jim Jackson owned the leather shop on the corner and kept his car in the open yard at its side. He came out of his office at once when she called him and listened to her explanation with tremendous interest. As I observed his slightly foxy face, pink under his sandy hair, my misgivings returned.

'I *can't* give you all this trouble,' I said. 'Let me take a taxicab.'

His eyes were bright and knowing and, under his secret amusement, kindly, I thought.

'Oh, it's no trouble,' he said, and if he had added 'It'll give her something to talk about for weeks,' he could not have made himself more clear. 'You sit in the back with her,' he went on, looking at his sister.

There was nothing for it. They had decided to take me and take me they did. If I'd not been so worried and embarrassed I should have found them comic. To all intents and purposes I was kidnapped. Jim refused point-blank to call at the school.

'It's not worth it,' he explained, treading on the accelerator as we passed the gates. 'It's only a mile and a half to the cottage. If he's not there we'll call coming back, unless you want me to run you to London.'

This last remark appeared to strike him as inordinately funny and he kept grinning to himself over it all the way to the golf course. I could see his face reflected in the high polish of the dashboard. I sat in a corner of the car with Amy very close to me and Izzy crouching on my knee. I did not want Victor to be injured, but I found that I was praying that we should find anything in the world rather than an unexplained and inexplicable visitor.

The cottage lay on the farther side of the golf course, at the end of a long overgrown lane tucked into a grove of lime trees. I had not seen it since my last visit in the early spring, when the trees had been bare. It was one of those very primitive lath-and-plaster hovels which look like something out of a fairy tale but turn out to be about as comfortable as a heap of rubble. When I came near I saw that a pink rose in full bloom had climbed all over the discoloured front, obliterating one window and even dislodging some of the tiles on the crazy roof. Ragged grass and untended flowers grew up almost to the eaves, and any passerby must have thought it derelict.

As Jim Jackson put his foot on the brake I leant forward and felt suddenly sick. The front door stood wide open. Amy Petty got out before I did, scrambling over me in her haste, but she did not cross the moss-grown path. She hesitated and looked back and waited for me. Jim too seemed in no hurry. He remained at the wheel, leaning back and watching me still with the same silly grin on his face. I let Izzy out onto the path and climbed after him, my knees weak.

'Victor!' I shouted. 'Vic-tor!'

I think we all held our breath. There was something quite horrible about the open door, a dark rectangle in the flowery wall.

No one answered. There was no sound at all save the hum of the bees in the limes and much twittering in the branches. I could see where the car had been driven round to the back of the house. The tall grass was beaten down in a line which ran past the open door to the derelict water butt in the corner. I followed it without speaking and Amy Petty came with me. We found the car. It had been driven into the bushes and was as completely hidden as one would have thought possible had one not known that the minute triangle of colour far away up the hill was a corner of Miss Bonwitt's garden. The car was quite damp inside and lay just as she had described it, the hood down and the rug hanging carelessly over the door. I hurried back with Amy at my heels and stepped into the cottage.

It was dark inside and cool. My feet sounded sharply on the brick floor. I was in the one reasonable room the place contained, a pleasant square place with a ceiling of whitewashed beams and a few pieces of old furniture scattered round the walls. There was a couch covered with a faded cotton spread, an armchair with a crumpled cushion in it, a gate-legged table and a rug. On the whitened chimney piece was an empty glass. A newspaper lay on the floor and Victor's bag of clubs leaned against a chest in the corner.

Amy Petty pushed past me and pounced on something lying in the armchair. I looked over her shoulder as she leant forward and I saw what it was, a half-filled packet of cigarettes.

I called again, startled by the tremor in my voice.

'Victor! Victor! Vic-tor!'

Once more everything was silent. Not a breath, not a sigh replied to me.

There was only one inner door, which led, as far as I recollected, to a back kitchen which looked and smelled like a dungeon. This door also stood open and I was advancing upon it when one of the most unnerving and horrible sounds I have ever heard in my life cut through the sleepy quiet of the afternoon. It was a long-drawn-out quavering howl which sent me starting back, while Amy made a noise in her throat. Immediately afterwards I knew what it was, Izzy of course. He had pottered on, investigating on his own account unheeded by either of us.

I rushed into the kitchen, which was minute and quite derelict, plaster falling off its walls and a trail of yellow-looking bindweed creeping in through a crevice under the old brick copper. I heard him howl again but I could not see Izzy.

It was a moment or so later when there was a movement in the darkest corner of all and a cupboard door which was swinging on a loose hinge opened wider as the little dog came backing out, his tail down and his ears flattened. He gave me one long meaning look and then, sitting back on his haunches, threw up his head so that the full sack of his hairy throat was showing and began to howl in earnest. Scotties are not noisy dogs, but when the occasion does arise they can hold their own with any breed on earth.

The noise was like an air-raid siren, horrible with the quaver of fear. Amid the wailing I heard from afar off the door of the Jacksons' car slam as Jim sprang out and the clatter as he blundered into the house behind us. Amy clutched me with a shaking hand.

'Look,' she commanded. 'Go on, look.'

As I pulled the cupboard door open Izzy stopped howling and began to bark, snapping at my dress and dancing about like a lunatic. It made me careful, which was fortunate because there was practically no floor to the deep recess and I could have stepped into the yawning hole at my feet.

It took me some seconds to make out what it was. It was the old iron pump with its corroded bucket which I saw first, I think, and then I looked down and the whole thing became frighteningly clear. The cupboard was not a cupboard but a door put over an alcove to hide the pump. It was a construction which is fairly usual in very old cottages. The iron pump handle came through the wood at the side so that one could use it while standing in the kitchen. The well was under the pump, its head level with the floor directly under the place where the bucket would hang. When it had been put in upwards of a hundred years before the cover had been made of elm three inches thick. The years of dripping water had won, however, and now the crazy lid, rotten as tinder wood, had disintegrated. A hinge tongue, sharp with years of rust, stuck out over the dark hole and attached to it was a six-inch sliver of newly rent wood.

I strained my eyes to see down into the darkness, and damp air, chill and revolting, reached my nostrils. Mercifully I was standing in my own light so I could see nothing but it was not difficult to imagine what might be floating in the dark bottom of that narrow pit. I felt a scream coming up in my throat and pressed my hands over my mouth to silence it, just as Jim pulled me out of the way.

The thing I remember best of the next ten minutes was the character displayed by the Jacksons. They were sound people, thoroughly country and thoroughly crude, but once they had got their own way, and once there was something obvious to be done wherein their motives could not be questioned, I found them willing, and in a domineering fashion good to me. Jim insisted on pushing us into the outer room while he went to the car for a torch. When he returned with it, it proved to be a typical Jackson possession, expensive and highly efficient. It was quite two feet long and threw a beam like a searchlight. He took it through into the kitchen while I sat in the chair and held Izzy. Amy stood with her back to the chimney, her face white as the lime-washed wall but with a queer satisfied expression in the curl of her tight lips.

We could only have waited for three or four minutes before Jim's high-pitched East Coast voice sounded from the inner room.

'Amy, come in here, girl, will you?'

She went hurrying in and I could hear them whispering for a bit before she returned with Jim following her, his face nearly as white as her own but his eyes bright with a shamed excitement.

Amy paused before me, her lips trying out phrases silently without uttering one of them. At last she gave up any attempt at finesse.

'He's in there, Mrs. Lane.'

I showed no astonishment. I am not half-witted and it had been perfectly obvious to me from the first moment I set eyes on the broken trap door that something of the sort must have occurred. I was stunned by the shock and I remember that the two silver bangles on my wrist were rattling together with a sound like fairy bicycle bells. But I was no longer astonished. That first reaction was over.

'How—how awful,' I said huskily.

Amy Petty looked at me for a long time and then she opened her bag and took out a clean handkerchief which she gave me gravely. I don't know why, but the precaution struck me as funny and to my horror—an explosive snort escaped me. To cover it I said I'd rather have a cigarette. She gave me one as if she was a hospital nurse inserting a thermometer, and her brother lit it for me with a great trembling hand which had curling yellow hairs and tiny beads of sweat standing out on it. He was so relieved that I was taking it quietly that he made the mistake of treating me as a disinterested spectator.

'There isn't above a foot of water in there!' he burst out. 'I see just what happened. Mr. Lane went to get himself a drop of water for the kettle, stepped on the little old door, which was as rotten as piecrust, and down he went, stunning himself most likely. He's lying in there, his head right under—I'd know him anywhere.'

I tried to stand up. My whole world and all its problems had taken a complete somersault and I felt as if I had nothing to hold on to.

Amy forestalled me. 'He went to get a drop of water,' she repeated thoughtfully. 'That's about it. We'll have to get him out. You go down to the clubhouse, Jim, for help. Just tell them quietly that there's been an accident. We don't want a whole lot of them coming up here. Tell—now I wonder who you'd better tell? Ring up Maureen.'

I heard her as if I were listening to a play and suddenly my common sense reasserted itself.

'That's no good at all,' I said. 'You'll have to fetch someone in authority. You'll have to get a doctor and—'

'The police!' Amy exclaimed as if she had had an original idea. 'That's it, Jim, ring up Uncle Fred South. He'll be at the Chief Constable's office as it's Friday.'

I was not surprised to hear her call the Superintendent 'Uncle,' and I remember reflecting with that part of my mind which was still working normally that quite probably he was their uncle. It would be positively queer if anyone totally unrelated to the Jacksons had any sort of responsible job in the town.

They argued with country thoroughness on the exact form of procedure suitable to the occasion, while I stood listening to them in a stunned sort of way and wondering why Victor should try to get himself a drop of water for the kettle, and where the kettle was now, and what he had intended to do with it when he had it full. There was no fire in the house. I also wondered why he should have stepped into the cupboard at all when the pump handle was outside.

There was no answer to any of these

questions and I made the mistake of thinking that they did not matter. I was absorbed by the one staggering fact: Victor was dead. I found I was desperately sorry for him but not in the least for myself. However awful this accident was, it still meant I was free, free to be myself and free to earn my living, free to live.

With Jim's departure, Amy became more of a menace. I found that I couldn't sit still in the room with her and I began to potter about, tidying up absently. It seemed that she felt the same way because she joined me and used the worn cushion cover as a duster. How we could have been so criminally stupid I do not know, except that we both accepted it as a fact that Victor had trodden on the trap door by mistake, and we were both tidy women to whom dust in that neglected room was an affront.

Amy found the carton. It was on the shelf behind the curtain near the couch. She took it down with both hands and, as I met her eyes, set it on the table. I recognised it at once, as would anyone who shopped in Tinworth. Bowers, the delicatessen people in West Street, put them up in dozens for people who wanted picnic luncheons. The cardboard box was covered with a willow-pattern design and tied with a scarlet cord. In comparison with everything else in the room it was very clean and new-looking. Without saying a word, Amy pulled the string and turned back the lid.

Inside there were two packets of sandwiches in cellophane, two plain cakes and two cream ones, two cardboard plates, two drinking cups and two apples. Everything was quite fresh. We stood on opposite sides of the table looking down at this forlorn meal, each waiting for the other to speak. After what seemed an interminable pause she took the initiative. When it came, her blunt remark epitomised Tinworth, its interest, its perception and its inescapable common sense.

'This'll cause *talk*,' she said.

'Yes,' I agreed sadly, but not with any bitterness. 'Poor Victor.'

Her small eyes opened wide at that. 'That's a funny attitude to take,' she remarked disapprovingly. 'No one thought you knew what he was. Well, there's no need to make more trouble than there is. I'll do this.'

While I watched she took out one cup and one plate, crushed them into the smallest possible wodge, and stuffed it into her leather handbag.

'That can go out of the window when Tim drives me home,' she explained coolly. 'Then I'll take the box and put it in Mr. Lane's car. Any man can take some food for himself if he's going to golf. You couldn't eat one of the apples, could you?'

'No,' I said, 'I couldn't.'

All the same, she removed an apple before retying the string. 'Two looks a lot for one person,' she explained. 'I'll take a bite out of this and break it up in the grass. You never know what that Miss Bonwitt might rake round and find.'

She went out on that line, taking the carton with her and leaving me alone in the cottage. I was astounded by her prompt handling of the embarrassing incident, and even admiring. I had not realised that she had it in her to do anything so charitable for anybody's reputation. I was grateful too. I was going to look pretty idiotic anyway after my crazy story of the telephone call. If there was concrete evidence of scandal as well, there *would* be an outburst of twittering.

Jim came back at last with the secretary of the club, two local members and a rope. The police were on their way out, he said, and meanwhile he'd had orders from 'Uncle' Fred South to drive Amy and me home at once so that she could put me to bed with tea and a hot bottle. It sounded a miraculous suggestion and I blessed the man, whoever he might be, for his kindness. However, it soon became rather obvious that neither Jim nor his sister had any intention of leaving the scene. Excitement of any kind was rare in Tinworth. Yet 'Uncle' appeared to have considerable authority and they were in a great pother about it until one of the club members, a pleasant youngster who had brought his own car, offered to drive me to the school and turn me over to Mrs. Williams.

I never went anywhere so willingly. Izzy and I curled up under a rug at the back of the car and shivered together. Shock makes me cold. I had learnt that in my A.R.P. days, but I'd never realised it before. My hands were icy, and to make things really horrible I had begun to imagine I could smell again the damp, chill reek which had come up from the well. I knew this was hysteria and I had got myself on a very tight rein, but when the boy drew up at the school gates I begged him not to bother to disturb Williams and swore through chattering teeth that I'd call him myself. He drove off gratefully and I fled down the path to the Headmaster's Lodging. I could not stand any more just then. I wanted to be alone more than anything in the world.

The hall struck cold when I opened the door and the first thing I saw was my own note to Victor, telling him to telephone the Superintendent about Rorke, propped up on the hall table. It might have been a hundred years since I had put it there, and it brought home the awful thing that had happened to Victor more vividly than anything else could have done. I snatched up the paper and crumpled it into a ball. I was glad of Izzy. Without him the house, empty and surrounded by empty buildings, would have been fearful. But he kept close to me, very much aware of all that was happening and very much on my side.

I went straight up to my bedroom. To run up and downstairs with boiling water seemed too difficult, so I thought I'd do without the tea and the bottle. I kicked off my shoes and pulled off my suit and only then remembered that all my things were packed. I found the right suitcase at last and got out my thickest dressing gown and some slippers. I gave Izzy some water and stripped the blankets off the bed. I thought if I could roll myself in them and curl up in a sort of bundle I might possibly get warm again. I also thought I might take a couple of the sedative sleeping pills which Dorothy had given me last holidays when she spent a week end with me while Victor was away. I did not remember packing these and I looked into the empty chest to see if the tiny phial could have slipped under the paper with which the drawers were lined.

The first thing I found was the roll of blotting paper which I had taken from Victor's desk, left there ready for me to show him as soon as he came in. I took it out and tore it up. I tore it into little square pieces and let them float down in a shower into the wastepaper basket. Poor Victor! At least we had both been spared one beastly half hour, and if Amy Petty of all people could protect his reputation so at least could I.

Then I went back to my search for the sleeping pills, but I could not find them anywhere and as I was growing colder and colder I got onto the bed and tried to doze. It was hopeless. My head had begun to throb violently and I could not stop shivering. Also, of course, I couldn't stop thinking. Finally I got up and went down to the dining room and lit the gas fire. Izzy came and sat on the rug with me and the heat slowly soaked into our bones.

I suppose it was about an hour later when the detective came. He made such a noise hammering at the door that I was quite angry with him when at last I got down to the hall to answer the knock. I had thought it must be Williams and the sight of the sturdy fresh-faced young man in the clumsy blue suit took me by surprise.

'Hullo,' I said, 'what is it?'

'It's the police, madam.' He was breathless, as if he had been running. 'I am a detective officer. Will you allow me to enter?'

Now even in England policemen do not talk quite like this unless they are very young or very new to the job. I decided he was both. He had taken a slanting glance at my old flannel dressing gown which covered me most decorously from chin to toe, and a deeper scarlet had stained his cheeks. I thought I should probably make him most comfortable by being as formal as he.

'Of course,' I said. 'I've been sitting by the fire in my room upstairs—my *dining* room. Would you like to come up there?'

He thought he would and clumped after me up the stairs, treading as cautiously as if he thought the parquet were glass. Once in the dining room, he sat down on the extreme edge of a hard chair and I took the low one by the fire.

'Well?' I enquired at last.

He cleared his throat. 'My orders were to stay with you, madam.'

'Stay with me?'

'Yes, madam. I understood that a Mrs. Williams from the lodge gates would be available to sit with us, and I called on her as I came in. But she, I understand, has been took bad and her husband is seeing to her. They have sent for a Mrs. Veal. Meanwhile I must ask you to stay where you are and await the Superintendent.'

He finished with a gasp and grew redder than ever.

I was puzzled and uneasy. It seemed to me very extraordinary that the Superintendent had not telephoned.

'Why does he want to see me?'

The full pink lips closed in a line. 'That, madam, I cannot say.'

'I see,' I murmured, and there was a long silence during which Izzy made the most thorough examination of the visitor's boots which any sleuth alive could have achieved.

The pause went on and on and finally I just had to say something or burst. I said, 'Have you been a detective long?'

'Two weeks.' His face was beetroot red. 'When we've done two years in the uniformed police we're allowed to volunteer for the plain-clothes branch. I volunteered.'

Because anything was better than the awful breathy silence I went on asking him about himself, and since, presumably, he had had no orders to prevent it he went on answering me. I learned that he was about twenty-two, was ambitious, was going to get married—nearly married, he said he was—and that he liked dogs but kept pigeons. Gradually I wore down his excessive formality and he hitched himself a little further back in his chair.

He was telling me how lucky he was to have been chosen for the exalted brotherhood of the County C.I.D. when he forgot his caution altogether.

'It's a privilege to serve under "Uncle," madam. You wouldn't believe. When he sent me out here today, I was as proud as if I'd got the Police Medal.'

I gaped at him. 'Good heavens,' I said, 'the Superintendent can't be your uncle too?'

That made him laugh and we were buddies. 'I didn't ought to have said that,' he confessed. 'It slipped out. That's the sort of thing you have to be careful about. One slip and you've got a black mark against you. It's a nickname the Superintendent's got. He's always been known by it, ever since he was first in the force. Everybody calls him by it to themselves. You can't help it. You'll find you will.'

'He sounds pleasant.'

'Pleasant?' My visitor's laugh was derisive. 'Not half! He's pleasant all right. He's wonderful.' He shook his head admiringly. 'You think he's your father and mother rolled into one and then—crash! He's seen right through you and bit your head off.'

I made no comment. There seemed little to say. The two-week detective was not looking at me. He was smiling with the fatuous delight of hero-worship.

'He thinks of everything, Uncle does,' he murmured. 'Look at today. The second they see the bullet wound he turns to me. "Root," he says, "this ain't accident, it's murder. You nip down to 'is wife, don't let her out of your sight until I come . . . oh, lor"!'

His dismay was as comic as anything I had ever seen in my life, but I had heard his words and every drop of blood in my body felt as if it had congealed. We sat staring at one another.

'You'll have to explain,' I said at last.

'I daren't, I daren't, m'm. They'll send me back to the uniformed branch and—'

'They'll sack you altogether if you don't use your head,' I said brutally. 'Come on, out with it. Do you realise you're talking about *my husband*? You can trust me not to give you away if you're not supposed to talk, but you certainly can't leave it like this.'

He licked his lips. Poor young man! He'd never make a policeman.

'I don't know much more, m'm,' he muttered. 'I went and told you about the lot, I'm afraid. That's all there was. We thought we were going to an accident but when we got there Sergeant Rivers—that's my sergeant—got down the well and tied a rope on the chap who was drowned. We heard him holler something as if he was surprised, and then we all pulled.' He considered me helplessly. 'This'll just about finish me, this will,' he mumbled wretchedly. 'Diane, that's my young lady, said I'd never be any good at this lark and it looks as if she's ruddy well right.'

'What happened when you pulled?'

'The body came up. That was when Uncle stepped forward. "Ullo ullo ullo," he says, and shouts down to the sergeant, "Got a gun down there, Charlie? Have a look for one, will you, now you're there," then he turns to me and tells me what I've just told you. If you tell . . .'

I did not hear any more.

Murder.

Victor murdered, shot presumably, although it sounded a spot diagnosis unless Detective Root was trying to spare me gruesome details. After the first paralysed moment I decided it was nonsense. It was too incredible. It simply couldn't have happened. Victor, of all people. Who would want to kill Victor?

I think it was that final question which

brought the position home to me. I think it was only when I asked it of myself that the elementary and obvious answer occurred to me. *I* was the person with real cause to hate him.

I totted up the motives as Tinworth knew or guessed them and added the new personality which Mrs. Raye had invented for me and had already discussed with her husband, the Chief Constable. And finally there was my own behaviour during the past thirty-six hours! Steadily, and with the relentlessness of a machine, my mind played the record back. There was my conversation with Mrs. Raye, my lie to Maureen. I'd actually told her that Victor was in the house! My lie to Mrs. Veal. My lie, heaven help me, even to the Superintendent. And then there was my bicycle ride. Who could swear where that had taken me? There was my reluctance when the Flower Club ladies wanted me to go to the cottage. There was my behaviour when I got there, the dusting and the tampering with the luncheon carton. As I sat remembering, it seemed as if every tiny thing I had done during the whole time could be misconstrued.

I felt beads of sweat coming out on my hairline and I stole a fearful glance at the detective, but he was lost in his own misery and sat there glumly, staring at his feet. On and on the dreadful catalogue of circumstantial evidence piled up in my mind until I was almost frantic. I found I was searching for replies to imaginary cross-questioning, explaining, twisting, trying to wriggle out of the net which I had woven for myself.

An hour passed, and then another, but there was no sign of the Superintendent. Nobody telephoned. The detective sat on, moody and silent, afraid to open his mouth.

At dusk Mrs. Veal arrived in a great state. She had not got the Williams' message until she had come in from 'the pic'chers' and 'could never forgive herself' for the delay. Fortunately for me, she diagnosed my condition as shock and not terror, and she bundled me into bed and made tea and brought hot-water bottles. She let Izzy out for run and promised to feed him, and she did not try to talk to me. I think she sized up the unfortunate Detective Root and decided that for information he was the better bet.

At first he wanted to sit in the room with me but she was so scandalised and so scathing that once more he failed in his duty and was prevailed upon to sit on the stairs outside. For a long time I could hear the drone of her questions and the wariness of his monosyllabic replies.

I drank the tea and lay looking at my suitcases. I could not tell whether it would be worse to unpack them again very quickly, or to say that I had thought that Victor and I were going on holiday at once. Either was impractical because I'd packed everything I owned, so I lay there and just thought.

* * *

The Superintendent arrived about midnight. His appearance was quiet and sudden, like an amiable demon's in a children's play. He made no sound at all. One moment I was dozing with my eyes closed against the bright light, and the next, when I opened them, there he was smiling at me from the middle of the room. As soon as I set eyes on him I knew who he was and why he had got his nickname. He was plump and grey-haired and amusingly ugly, with a face which could have been designed by Disney. His eyebrows were tufts over bright little eyes which danced and twinkled and seemed ever stretched to their widest. His old tweed clothes were a little too tight for him, so that he looked disarmingly shabby, and his step was the lightest and most buoyant I have ever seen. The moment I saw him I felt reassured.

He waited for the effect to sink in and the he said, 'Awake?'

'Yes. Yes, I haven't slept.' I scrambled into a sitting position. 'I know who you are. I've been waiting for you. What have you found out?'

He spun round and flicked on every remaining light, and, in continuation of the same movement took up a chair and sat down astride it so that he was looking at me from over its back.

'Everything,' he replied, and his movements had been so swift that there did not seem to have been a pause between question and answer. 'How much do *you* know?'

I remembered the unhappy Detective Root, at this moment trembling on the stairs no doubt.

'I know my husband was found in the well.'

His brows shot up, but his eyes still twinkled, intelligent, worldly, bright with secret entertainment.

'But you found him, didn't you?'

'Mr. Jackson found him. I looked first but I hadn't a torch.'

'Nor you had. A very nasty thing to happen to a young girl. A dreadful experience. I'm not going to ask you if you were fond of him because you won't want to be asked anything like that yet. It's too soon. It'll only upset you.'

He paused, but I did not speak and he nodded as though with satisfaction.

'Do you want to know what happened to him?'

'Yes,' I said. 'Yes, of course I do.'

'He was shot.' He pulled out the information like a rabbit from a hat and held it up for comment.

'Shot . . .' I echoed. The light was full in my eyes and I blinked as I spoke.

'With his own gun.'

This was another rabbit from the hat and this one did astound me.

'With . . . ? Are you saying he shot himself?'

He smiled broadly. It was the first time I had seen him do that, but I was to find out that he did it all the time. He smiled if he was condoling with the bereaved, or giving evidence in court. It was said to have cost him a career in the Metropolitan C.I.D. and to be the reason why he was still a provincial.

'I'm not saying anything.'

'But he can't have!' I protested.

'Why not?'

'Because he wouldn't. He wasn't that sort of person.'

'No,' he agreed, and made a gesture with his hands as if he was throwing away some little trifle he had picked up and had decided was useless. 'No, and he wasn't an acrobat either, so he didn't shoot himself through the back of the head whilst falling down a well. That's right.'

'Then someone else shot him.'

He nodded, holding me with those bright dancing eyes.

'Who?' I demanded. 'Do you know?'

He nodded again, still with the same expression. For the first time I began to feel afraid of him. There was something sinister in that knowing twinkle with its undercurrent of irrepressible gaiety. Almost I expected him to invite me to guess who. By that time I had begun to notice that he was forcing me to do all the talking. Detective Root had said something about him. What was it? 'You think he's your father and mother and then—crash! he's bitten your head off.'

I grew very still. Perhaps he did suspect me and was trying to make me give myself away. My lips were very dry and I licked them.

He noted the fact openly, with another nod of satisfaction.

'What can I tell you?' I murmured at last.

'Nothing.' He got up and moved about the room, still keeping his eyes on me. It was an odd performance and I could not think what it was in aid of until I realised that he was simply seeking the position in which he could best see my face. 'Nothing,' he repeated. 'Nothing now. I'm going to leave you to sleep. That old woman can stay the night and she can make you some hot grog. All this tea, very lowering. Doesn't get you anywhere. I shall leave my poor little boy with the great thick boots and the great thick head here too. He can chase away visitors and you can sleep. Good night.'

I was amazed and utterly relieved. 'Good night,' I said breathlessly.

He walked to the door, paused with his hand on the knob as if he'd suddenly recollected something, and walked back into the room to the exact spot on the carpet which he had just left.

'We pulled him in,' he remarked, still beaming. 'I thought you'd like to know. He was very gentlemanly about it. Came at once without any bother. Hopped on the train with the sergeant and they were down here by suppertime.'

I hadn't the faintest idea what they were talking about and I gaped at him like an idiot.

'Who?'

'The young feller we want.' The country voice shook with suppressed exuberance and his gaze never once left my face. 'The young man you slipped your husband's gun to. The lad you curled your hair for. The doctor fellow who couldn't bear to see you so unhappy. I hear he sent you some flowers this morning to tell you it was safely done . . . little blue flowers meaning "success." Pretty idea, really. I like that. But I'm not condoning it, mind. He's been a very bad boy and he'll have to pay for it. There's no getting round that.'

PART THREE

The Superintendent's voice died away but the words hung terrifyingly in the quiet room. For a long time I could not even believe that I had heard them, or that they meant what I thought. I sat up in the bed, looking at him woodenly and feeling that the world had come abruptly to an end.

'Well?' he enquired at last.

I just sat and shook my head at him, too appalled at first even to protest. He was watching my face eagerly and my silence seemed to puzzle him.

'Go on,' he insisted. 'Admit it. It's true, isn't it?'

'No.' I got the word out at last and, having done so, did not seem able to stop saying it. 'No, no, no.' I knew I was shouting and could not keep quiet. His expression changed immediately and his voice rose with authority.

'Look out, that's not the way. That's not the way. Pull yourself together.'

'I'm sorry,' I muttered, 'but you were *too* wrong.'

His chin shot up and his eyes were narrow. 'What exactly do you mean by that? Take your time. Explain yourself. I'm here to listen.'

I did my best but things seemed to be happening to me. For one thing, I suddenly became so tired than I could hardly speak at all. I heard myself ploughing on hopelessly.

'It's not only rubbish, it's wicked rubbish,' I was saying wearily. 'You could ruin his career with your silly mistakes. You've got it utterly wrong.'

At that point I realised I was making it sound as though it wasn't Andy because it was me, but I was too exhausted to explain. My head fell forward and I straightened up with an effort and made myself look at him.

He was eyeing me very curiously and I could see him hesitating in the middle of the room. He looked ridiculous, like a captive balloon swaying there on the balls of his feet. It went through my mind that he was trying to choose between two entirely different courses of action and at last he came to a decision and pointed a long finger at me.

'This has upset you a thousand times more than the death of your husband. Why?'

I remember making a gesture of helplessness as my eyes widened and my vision began to blur.

'Well,' I said brokenly, 'it's come on top of it.'

The point got home to him. I felt the impact of his comprehension as clearly as if it had been a physical contact. He stepped back, made a startled cluck of a sound and immediately, like a conjuring trick, his personality changed back to the avuncular gnome again.

'Now I'll tell you what,' he said. 'We'll both

have a spot of steak-and-kidney pudding. You haven't had any dinner, that's what's wrong with you. I haven't either. We shall be getting ourselves upset. Let's have a bite and talk later.'

The extraordinary thing was that he actually had some steak-and-kidney pudding, in fact he had a whole meal, enough for a family, packed up in an old-fashioned open basket covered with a cloth. It was down with the police car, being kept hot on the radiator, and he had it brought up into our dining room. I put on my dressing gown again and had some with him, and Detective Root waited on us, with Mrs. Veal hovering and whispering in the passage outside. Izzy was brought in and he had some as well.

Uncle Fred South explained this latter-day miracle with a nonchalance which, I was to learn, was all part of his legendary personality. His wife did not like him to miss his meals, he said, and now that he was so high up in the police hierarchy that he could afford to be unconventional he got her to send his dinner out to him whenever he had to stay late at the office. He mentioned cheerfully that at the moment his office was downstairs. He smiled at me confidingly.

'She *likes* doing it,' he said.

It was a peculiar pudding of a hard old-fashioned kind and it had dried fruit and heaven knows what else in it, besides meat, but

I think it saved my life. The pause snapped the tension and my feet touched ground again. It also gave me time to think. I could see that our only hope, Andy's and mine, was for me to tell the truth, the whole truth and nothing but the truth, and to be double quick about it, but my fear was that even so it wasn't going to be good enough. In my efforts to save the appearances of my 'ordinary' marriage I had made some colossal blunders, and by making them I had involved one of the few people I had to care about in the world. I decided to let the Superintendent talk first and we had our meal almost in silence.

He was eating some very strong green cheese, which he had pressed me to share but had seemed relieved when I refused, when he looked up suddenly and asked me if I knew Izzy was deaf. I said I did not think so.

'He is. A little.' The round man nodded at me. He was glowing again, the meaningful twinkle which I had grown to fear reappearing in his eyes. 'It's not much, probably only a bit of wax. We'll take him down to Mr. Cooper the vet and get his ears syringed sometime.' As usual, he made me feel that there was some hidden significance behind this statement which he expected me to follow and share, and his next remark was equally bewildering. 'Have you ever been to the zoo, Mrs. Lane?'

'The—the zoo?'

'That's right. In London. They've got a

beehive there in a glass case. You can stand and see everything in it, the bees all moving and working and eating and talking and quarrelling.' He paused again, and again the alarming twinkle invited me to understand and be as entertained as he was. When I continued to look at him blankly, he laughed. 'I always go and look at it,' he said. 'It reminds me of home. Just like Tinworth.'

At last I saw what he was talking about and it was like suddenly understanding a new and frighteningly economical language. I saw that he was telling me that I had not a hope of hiding anything from him, and that the gossipy interest of Tinworth in everything and everybody had ensured that every move I had made and every word I had spoken had gone back to him with the speed of light. *I* was in a glass case, that's what he was saying. I also thought I understood what he meant about Izzy. The dog had not barked when I had thought we were alone with Detective Root.

'How long have you and your people been in the house?' I demanded.

His twinkle grew approving as if I were a pupil who was coming along nicely.

'Hours and hours,' he said cheerfully. 'You gave us a lot of work with that piece of blotting paper from your husband's desk. It's not complete yet. What do you think we are—jigsaw puzzle experts? What was on it?'

I looked down. 'Part of a letter Victor had

131

written to some woman, arranging to meet her yesterday.'

He was not in the least suprised. 'Did it say where?'

'No.'

'Did you read it with a looking glass?'

'No, I can read that kind of writing.'

'Can you? That's useful. Done a bit of printing—at school, I suppose. When did you tear it up?'

"This afternoon, when I came in.'

'Ah.' I'd told him something he didn't know at last. 'When you knew he was dead, eh? That's why it was upstairs. What were you saving it for? Divorce evidence?'

'I don't know much about divorce evidence,' I said. 'I was going to show it to him as soon as he came in.'

'In that case why did you move it?'

'Because I didn't know when he was coming in. I didn't want it to get tidied up or inked over, but I wasn't going to sit by it.'

He grunted, not too pleased. 'It's a good story.'

'It's not a story, it's true.'

'All right,' he said testily, 'I'm not questioning you.'

'But you are.'

'Now look'—he pointed his table knife at me—'I am doing no such thing and don't you forget it. You and I are having a quiet preliminary chat. Once I want to start questioning you I've got to caution you, and once I caution you I've got to charge you, and once I charge you I've got to bring you up before a magistrate pretty toute suite. That's the law of the land. You don't want that, do you?'

'No.'

'And you want to find out who shot your husband, don't you?'

'Of course.'

'Well then, don't be so silly. Let's go on chatting away about it and see where we get to. Did you enjoy your bike ride yesterday afternoon?'

I leant forward impulsively. 'I've been thinking about that. The gardener saw me go and Williams saw me come back, but I shall never be able to prove where I went.'

'Why not?'

'Because I only went to the river.'

He settled back in his chair with a cigarette, loosening his belt very discreetly, convinced, I am certain, that he was unobserved.

'Tell us about it,' he suggested. 'We've got all night.'

There was very little to tell, but I made it as circumstantial as I could. It did not sound very convincing even to me, and when I came to the end I said so.

'I hardly expect you to believe this,' I finished lamely.

The knowing gleam returned to his eyes. 'I

don't believe you could invent anything worse as an alibi,' he admitted cheerfully. 'So you just went peacefully to sleep under a willow, did you? And very nice too.'

'I didn't see any willows that I remember,' I said uncertainly.

'No,' he agreed, 'you wouldn't. There aren't any there. Funny thing, it's the one stretch of bank where they won't grow. Well, that doesn't get us anywhere, does it? Suppose we get back to the Headmaster, Mrs. Lane. When did you see him last?'

'On Wednesday night.'

He looked up at that but did not ask the obvious question about Thursday morning. Instead he said casually, 'I don't suppose you can remember what his last actual words to you were?'

I remembered them very well, but I hesitated. As well as being distasteful in the extreme, the prospect looked horribly dangerous. He was waiting, however, and I took the plunge. I remember feeling that my only hope was to shut off every part of my mind except the actual bit I should need to recollect, and go on steadily regardless of everything except the exact truth.

'We had been talking about the holidays,' I began. 'Victor said, "My dear child, I cannot put it any more plainly to you. I will discuss the matter later. Now I am very tired and there is still a great deal of school business to be done.

If you will excuse me I will go to bed. Good night."'

I raised my eyes to find Uncle Fred South regarding me fishily. His mouth had fallen open a little.

'Quarrelling?'

'Not exactly.'

'I see.' It was quite clear that he did nothing of the kind. 'Did he always talk to you like that?'

I felt myself growing red again. 'He talked to everybody like that.'

'I know he did. But . . . were you alone?'

'Yes, we were in here.'

'I see,' he said again, still in the same unconvinced way. 'Was there anything special about the holiday?'

There was nothing to do but to tell him and to make it as factual as the bicycle ride. I found myself talking very fast to get it over.

'Yes, there was. At least, I thought so. I had not seen much of Victor during the term, although we both lived here. The school took up all his time. I asked him about the vacation several times but he never had a moment to discuss it. On Wednesday, when the school was actually closing, the matter seemed to me to be rather urgent, so I waited for him when he came up from his late-night session in his study and I asked him again. He told me he thought he should have to go on his usual climbing expedition after all, and asked me if I couldn't go to stay with friends.'

I stopped, but Uncle Fred South was quietly firm.

'Go on,' he said. 'I knew him, you know. I've known him for years, much longer than you have. Just tell me what happened.'

'Well,' I said, 'I told him I did not want to do that, and that we had been married for six months and seemed to be still virtual strangers. I said I thought we ought to go away together. He said I was talking like a novelette and that he was very tired and would see me in the morning. I attempted to insist, because I wanted the thing settled, and he then said what I've just told you. That's all.'

'But he didn't see you in the morning?'

'No. When I came down at the usual time he had already breakfasted, and when I'd had mine he was with Mr. Rorke in his study. I went down the town to get away from it all and when I came back he had gone. I never saw him again.'

The Superintendent stubbed out his cigarette. His eyes had lost their twinkle but not their knowingness.

'And when you went down the town you met your old sweetheart and told him all your troubles and how you were neglected, and that your husband was unfaithful as well . . .'

'No.' I was too earnest even to be angry with him. 'No, I didn't even know then that Victor had even been faintly interested in any

136

woman.'

He sat back, throwing up his hands. 'Oh, come, Mrs. Lane,' he said, 'think again.'

I stuck to my guns. 'I did not,' I insisted. 'I can understand now that the whole of this beastly town must think me demented for not knowing as much as everybody else did about Victor, but they've all known him longer than I have, and besides, there is one great difference between us.'

'What's that?'

'They *wanted* to know something unpleasant about him. I didn't, naturally. I'd married him.'

He regarded me with a new respect. 'You're not quite the gentle little mug—hrmmph! party you look, are you? When did you find out?'

'Mrs. Raye told me, or conveyed it, rather, when she drove me home from the High Street after I'd said good-bye to Andy. Later on I saw the blotting paper.'

'Oho!' said Uncle Fred South with sudden triumph. 'Oho! That explains quite a bit.'

'What? The blotting paper?'

'No, no. Mrs. Raye spilled the beans, did she? She didn't mention that, my lady didn't. Well, well, so she's got a conscience after all. Perhaps I'd better give you this lot.'

He felt in his coat pocket and pulled out a collection of envelopes.

'These kept coming for you all the evening,' he explained blandly. 'We had to take 'em in at the lodge or you'd have come downstairs and found us at work. We notified the exchange to divert all telephone calls to the station for the same reason. You read these and you'll find out something about this beastly town, as you call it, that you didn't know before.'

'What's that?' I enquired warily.

'That it's only uncharitable in word,' he said with unexpected seriousness. 'It's all right when it comes to deeds, sound as a bell.'

I did not answer him. I had opened the first of the letters and its contents had caught me unawares.

Dear Mrs. Lane,

I thought I must just write to you and let you know that we are here. If there's absolutely anything that Percival or I can do, from walking the dog to running you to London, do please let us know.

Ever yours sincerely,
Betty Roundell

There were so many of them, all in the same strain, from Hester Raye's 'Dear Elizabeth, Don't be frightened. It will be ALL RIGHT. Love from Hester' to dear Miss Seckker's three pages in a fine gothic hand.

My dear Mrs. Lane,

My brother has had to go to London to visit poor Mr. Rorke, who has been taken to hospital, or he would be at your side. *I have been to the lodge gates myself but have not yet been able to gain admittance. Pray believe me my dear girl, when I say that I am thinking of you all the time and sending you my heartfelt sympathy. I hope that you will come here as soon as it is permitted. We have three cats but they are good and your little dog will be more than welcome . . .*

I looked up at the Superintendent, who was watching my shaking hands.

'You've had these steamed open,' I accused him.

His eyes were at their small widest and the twinkle was bland with meaning. He nodded shamelessly and said, 'I never.'

'They're very kind,' I murmured huskily.

'More than kind, downright interfering,' he observed. 'You know why we've had to sit up all night? The Chief, Colonel Raye, has sent to London for his own solicitor to represent you. He's a terrible big guy, name of Sir Montague Grenville. The Colonel didn't think you ought to be in the hands of a local man. Thought it might not be fair. He'll be down first thing in the morning and then I don't suppose I'll be able to say how-d'you-do to you without him sitting there listening. That's why I had to get such a move on. Still, if Mrs. Raye felt guilty about what she hinted to you, that explains that. Very human, people are, especially women.'

I had no time to comment on this extraordinary and in some ways outrageous statement, for just then a detective I had never seen before came into the room and there was a muttered conference. Uncle Fred South put on a pair of spectacles and eyed me over the top of them.

'I've got a transcript here of the items from the blotting paper. I see the one you mean.' He nodded a dismissal to the detective, who went out, leaving us alone again. It was quiet in the room and, despite the fire, cold. Uncle Fred South had undergone one of his changes. Now that he was off guard for a minute or so I could see him as he was without the mannerisms, a single-minded, kindly but utterly inexorable machine for finding out the wrongdoer and bringing him to justice. He was not satisfied with me. I could smell it rather than see it. I knew I had shaken and puzzled him, but as yet he was unconvinced.

'You see, Mrs. Lane,' he said suddenly, just as if he had been following my thought and was answering it, 'someone shot your husband between one o'clock and four o'clock yesterday afternoon. Someone holding Mr. Lane's own gun forced him back through the door of the kitchen, across the floor towards the cupboard door, which was probably standing open. Whether your husband stepped in there with some idea of shutting the door on himself as a protection, or whether he just went blindly where he could to get away from the gun, we do not know, but at any rate the rotten floor gave way under him and more than likely he stepped back involuntarily, turning his head towards this new danger. At that moment someone fired. The bullet entered the back of the neck and ploughed its way up into the skull, the body plunged down into the water, and someone threw the gun in after him.'

He made it all so horribly vivid that I shrank back into the chair. I had an instinct to cover my eyes but I controlled it and kept staring at him.

'I didn't,' I said.

'I never suggested that you did,' he reminded me gently. 'I don't even think you were there. But I want you to realise one thing. The deed has been done. Someone shot him in cold blood while he was running away. There was no fight, so there's no question of self-defence. Understand?'

'Yes, I understand, but to suggest that Andy—'

'Wait.' He held up a hand to stop me. 'Wait. Don't say anything until I've finished. Just give your mind to what I'm telling you. There's the killing, that's the first thing. Then there's your behaviour. You've told lies to everybody about your husband's whereabouts. You've attempted to destroy evidence. You've packed your bags. And on the night after your husband's died you sat up beautifying yourself for the first time since your marriage. Also, you were one of the few people who could have got possession of your husband's gun.'

'Anybody in the whole school could have got possession of that gun if Victor left it where it was when I saw it last term,' I protested.

He shook his head at me. 'I told you to wait till the end. Now I want you to think of Dr. Andrew Durtham's behaviour. He comes to a town where the girl he loves is unhappily married to another man. He knows she is there, mind. He takes a locum's job there, deliberately. He meets her "accidentally" in the street and they take a long drive together round and round the town, talking their heads off. The very same day he drives out to the golf club, where he is made an honorary member. He lunches there with the doctor who has sponsored him. One of the other members who is lunching there also is your husband. In the bar afterwards the two men are introduced and stay chatting for a few minutes. The deceased was in good spirits. Dr. Durtham was noticed to be downcast.'

'Victor lunched at the club?' I burst out, but again he silenced me.

'Quiet. After a while the deceased says good-bye and drives off in his car, only a few hundred yards as we know now, to his own cottage, where he secretes the vehicle. Meanwhile Dr. Durtham, who is noticeably preoccupied, refuses a round of golf but goes off alone, ostensibly to walk round the course, which he has never seen before. He is out till nearly half past five, returns to the clubhouse, picks up his car and drives back to Tinworth, where he makes arrangements to leave the town, the job and everything immediately. In the morning he buys a bowl of blue flowers alleged to mean "success" and delivers them at the school lodge, where he calls to see a last patient. Now what have you got to say?'

'Andy didn't shoot Victor.'

'How do you know?'

'There was no reason why he should. Andy came here to tell me what he thought of me for jilting him, not to make love to me.'

'I've only got your word for that.'

'Have you? Haven't you asked Andy?'

'It's the story you arranged between you, is it?'

'Oh, nonsense!' I was suddenly and recklessly angry with him. 'This is absurd. I don't know why Andy went to the golf course, but I don't see where else a stranger to Tinworth would go on a half day, do you? How would he find the cottage anyway, and if he did, why would he kill Victor? He certainly isn't in love with me any more.'

'Are you sure?'

'Of course I'm sure.' The words were pouring out of my mouth and I was saying things I did not know I knew. 'Andy came

143

down here to get me out of his system. When he saw me I'd changed and he probably wondered what he'd been making all the fuss about. This must have upset him and so I suppose he thought he'd clear out and get away from it all. I expect he thought I must be in love with Victor or I'd never put up with him.'

'And were you, Mrs. Lane?'

'No,' I said slowly, and the words were a revelation to me too, 'no, I was just out of love with love. I was trying to make do without it.'

He cocked a bright eye at me. 'And then you suddenly saw the light and . . .'

'No. Superintendent, you're behaving as though Andy and I and Victor were alone in the world. What about all the other people? To begin with, what about the girl?'

Uncle Fred South was leaning over the table, his clown's face grave and the twinkle absent from his circular eyes.

'The girl?' he began. 'You're still harping on that message on the blotter, are you? That's not very conclusive evidence, you know. How d'you know it referred to this month even?'

'But he expected someone,' I insisted. 'In fact, since he had lunch at the clubhouse it must have been she who brought the picnic box, not realising he would have eaten, you see.'

'The picnic box!' He bounced half out of his chair at that. 'I knew there was something funny about that great parcel of food in the car. You did that! You moved it! What other evidence have you been monkeying about with, eh? You and your crazy face-saving which doesn't fool anybody. Out with it!'

'I'm sorry,' I said, 'I thought Mrs. Petty would have told you about that—she seems to have mentioned everything else.'

He stiffened like a dog at a rathole. 'Amy Petty? Was she in that?'

I told him exactly what had happened over the box and he took me back again and again until the entire incident had been reconstructed in the most minute detail.

'Huh!' he said at last. 'So Amy destroyed the extra cup and plate, did she? And why did you suppose she did that?'

'To save scandal. We didn't dream he'd been murdered.'

A crow of laughter with no mirth in it whatever escaped him and his round eyes were wary for a change.

'How long have you known Amy? Six months, eh? I've known her thirty years. She married a lad I loved like a son and I always reckon he died to get away from her. Caught pneumonia and died just to get a bit of peace.' He was genuinely moved, I saw to my astonishment. Forgetting himself entirely, he leant across the table and wagged a finger at me. 'I said to him on his deathbed, "George," I said, "make the effort, old son. Hang on, hang on." He smiled at me and said, "What's the use, Pop? I'm tired of her and her darned family." Then he died. That's Amy.'

He smiled at me with surprising bitterness, remembered who I was and where we were and pulled himself up abruptly.

'I ought not to have said all that,' he said seriously. 'That's what's wrong with knowing a town inside out. The people become too real to you. But Amy's a Jackson and to a Jackson no one matters twopenn'orth of cold coffee but another Jackson. Amy was saving scandal all right.'

A great light broke over me and at last I saw what ought to have been obvious to me from the very beginning, but which had been completely mysterious because I did not want to know of its existence.

'Maureen,' I said aloud. 'Maureen. The scandal last winter was about Victor and Maureen?'

Uncle Fred South nodded casually. That this might be news to me did not seem to occur to him.

'The family was just banding together to make him marry her,' he went on, 'when along he comes with a brand-new wife who was much more his style, much prettier, much more polite, and without a family behind her. They were always a bit slow, the Jacksons, slow off the mark. They can't help it. It's the country in them.' He grinned. "They'd have got rid of him, banded together and forced him to quit the town if it hadn't been for Maureen. She was angry, but she couldn't do without him seemingly. Well, well, we'll see if Maureen bought that picnic box. Maisie Bowers is a sharp kid. She'll remember if she served her.'

I was crouching over the table with my head between my clenched hands. Many things which before had been mysterious were now devastatingly clear. But not the main problem. This development seemed to make that more dark than ever. Amy Petty had forced me to make the discovery of Victor's death. As I looked back that seemed so very obvious that I was amazed I had not spotted it at the time. I remembered her pallid smile of triumph when Jim had gone to find the torch, and understood it at last.

'But in that case why did she come round here with someone asking for Victor?' I said aloud. 'If Maureen shot him, why . . . ?'

'She didn't shoot him.' Uncle Fred South spoke as flatly as if he had inside information from some heavenly headquarters.

'Well then, if a Jackson shot . . . ?'

'No Jackson ever shot anybody.' Again he made the statement sound irrefutable fact. 'They'll band together and beggar a man and drive him to suicide or out of his mind. They'll have their revenge on him if they consider he's crossed them and they'll never let up if they take it to the third or fourth generation, but they'd never shoot anybody, or poison them or bang them on the head like you or I might.'

'Why not?'

'Because they're very just, upright people and the backbone of this here nation,' he said primly. 'Did you say Maureen wasn't alone when she came round here in the night? Who was with her? Was it Amy?'

'It could have been she.' As soon as he made the suggestion I felt sure he was right. 'Whoever it was stayed in the shadow and I assumed it was a man. Maureen was very upset. I thought she was giggling.'

He moved his head up and down very decidedly once or twice.

'It was Amy,' he said. 'That's about it. Maureen would go to Amy and they'd discuss what to do. Finally Maureen would get her way and they'd come round to make sure.'

'Sure of what?' I demanded, completely foxed by him and his lightning reconstructions.

'Sure he wasn't down the well,' said Uncle Fred South calmly, 'the well with the broken trap door. That's what Maureen found when she went in to meet him yesterday afternoon with her picnic box. That wasn't Tinworth's idea of a lunch, young lady, that was tea, or a cocktail snack to be washed down from a flask. Depend upon it, that's what happened. Perhaps she waited around for a bit and then got to exploring, but when she saw the broken

148

trap, well, it's my bet she wasn't in the place two seconds after that.'

'But he might have been in there alive.'

'Not a hope. Maureen would know that, and she'd be off like a streak so that no one tried to connect her with any trouble. Once she was safe, then she'd start thinking. Amy is the one she would tell. Yes, come to think of it, Amy is obvious.'

'How can you possibly know all this?' I demanded. 'You're jumping to conclusions, just like you were about me and Andy.'

He acknowledged the thrust with a bow of his close-cropped head and for a second the twinkle returned to his eyes.

'I know the Jacksons like my wife knows the ingredients she puts in her cooking,' he said. 'Show her anything that comes out of the oven and she'll tell you every item that's in it, and what was done to them before they were put in there. Perhaps I don't know you and the doctor quite so well, but I'm learning. What sort of footing are you two on? Tell me that and I could tell you things about yourselves that neither of you know.'

'But I've told you,' I began helplessly.

He beamed at me with unexpected friendliness. 'You've been very frank, more than Amy has, the vixen. I've a good mind to go and get that madam out of her bed. Fancy her thinking she could put one over on me after all these years!' He got up and stretched himself. 'Would you be afraid to stay here alone tonight?'

'No,' I said. 'I've got Izzy and it's almost morning.'

He seemed still undecided. 'The old woman had to go home but she'll be back very early. I'd leave one of my boys with you but I need 'em all.'

'It's perfectly all right,' I said firmly. 'I'd like to be alone.'

He pounced on that. 'There's no point in you prowling round the house looking for more evidence to destroy. We've been over it with a toothcomb. What we've missed doesn't exist.'

'I don't want to look for anything. I've told you the truth. All I want to do is to go to bed.'

He appeared to come to a sudden decision. 'All right. All right. Hurry upstairs and pop under the blanket. You can lock your door if you like. Take the dog. He's a nice little chap, likes me.'

He bent to scratch Izzy's ears and laughed when the little animal flattened them and shied away from him. I gathered the dog up in my arms and stumbled upstairs, too tired to be anything but thankful to get away. My room was very tidy and I knew at once that it had been searched. All my suitcases had been opened. I was sure of it because they were fastened so neatly, the straps pulled so tight.

I got into bed, put Izzy on the end of it, and

lay down. Then I turned off the light.

Downstairs there was considerable movement. The police, who had arrived as silent as ghosts, were leaving like the boys at end of term. Although I was at the top of the house I could hear their boots on the parquet and twice the door slammed. My window was wide open and I heard them leave one after the other. I heard the Superintendent's voice in the courtyard and another which I was pretty certain was Detective Root's. Outside the sky was brightening rapidly and from far away over the fields the unearthly cry which is cockcrow echoed in the quiet air. I heard the police cars drive off and the sound of their engines fading away down Tortham Road. Then everything was silent.

I was too exhausted even to sleep and I was horribly afraid. While I had been listening to the Superintendent talking about the Jacksons I had fooled myself into thinking that I had convinced him, and that everything was going to be all right, but the moment I was alone the full frightfulness of the situation returned and I remembered his summing up word for word, as if I were hearing it over again. Someone had killed Victor in cold blood. I had lied again and again concerning his whereabouts. Andy had been wandering about in the vicinity of the murder at the time when it had been committed.

I lay there letting the thoughts turn over and

over in my mind until the whole story became distorted and out of touch with reality. It was the crime itself which became so utterly monstrous. I thought of a dozen unlikely explanations for it. Once, even, I wondered if Andy could conceivably have got into some extraordinary set of circumstances in which he had somehow fired the shot. Yet in the unreal, half-light world of terror I knew that was absurd. It was far easier to imagine that in a fit of amnesia I had done it myself. The problem remained.

Meanwhile the sky grew slowly brighter and the early morning sounds began to multiply in the world outside. I don't know how long it was before I first heard the car. The noise was very faint at first, a far-off petrol engine, not very new, pounding towards me through the dawn. It got louder and louder and I could hear it roaring up the road.

The squeal of brakes as it stopped took me by surprise, it sounded so close. Then a door slammed loudly and in the clear silent air I heard feet on the gravel in the drive. They came closer and closer until with a sharp, swift tattoo they found the stones of the courtyard. Someone was striding quickly and noisily into the school with as much assurance as if it belonged to him. Izzy sat up, his ears pricked, but he did not bark and I wriggled up on the pillows, my heart thudding so noisily I could hardly hear anything else. Under my window the footsteps paused and there was a moment of complete quiet until, quite suddenly, there came a tremendous banging at the front door, sharp, hard knocking as though from a man in a rage.

Izzy began to bark at last and I leapt out onto the floor just as the very last voice in the world which I had expected came up to me, loud and unmistakable.

'Liz!' Andy was shouting at the top of his voice. 'Liz, where are you? What are you doing in this darned morgue alone? Liz!'

I put my head out of the window. My eyes were smarting but I was half laughing too, I was so glad to hear him.

'Andy, be quiet. You'll wake the neighbourhood. Here I am.

'Well then, for heaven's sake,' he exclaimed, turning a relieved face up to me in the faint light, 'come down and let me in. What do they want to do, turn you into a raving lunatic?'

'I'm all right,' I assured him. 'Wait a minute.'

I raced down the stairs through the silent house, with Izzy flip-flopping behind me, got the door open, drew Andy in and took him up to the dining room. It was warm in there and the cloth was still on the table, although the remains of the meal had been cleared. I opened a window to air the place and I recall that my hands were so unsteady I could scarcely find the catch.

Andy was silent, which was unusual in him, and when he helped me with the window I was aware of the suppressed anxiety that possessed him.

'It was madness to leave you up here alone,' he said. 'I can't understand them.'

'I'm all right now I know you are,' I admitted frankly. 'I thought they'd arrested you.'

'Arrested me?' His dark hair appeared to bristle as he turned towards me, lean and rakish, his skin drawn tight with weariness. 'Did they tell you that?'

'Not exactly. They conveyed it.'

He grunted. 'They think they're being clever, don't they? I've been invited to talk, that's all so far. But they can't pin anything on me. How can they? I'd only met the man for five minutes.'

I was not convinced. 'You don't understand,' I began, 'they've got it all worked out. They think I rode out to the golf course on a bicycle, gave you Victor's gun, and—'

He was standing close beside me and at the moment, without any preamble whatever, he turned and put his arms round me and kissed me very hard. I don't remember any surprise, only an intense relief. It was as if a load I did not know I was carrying had slid off my shoulders forever. I kissed him back and put my hands behind his head to hold him to me.

We stood quiet for a long time. At last he

said earnestly, 'I love you, Liz. I'm crazy about you. I must be or I shouldn't be here now. It's gone on for a long time, too, or I shouldn't have come to Tinworth in the first place. You love me just as desperately, you know that, don't you?'

'Yes,' I said, still in the same strange liberated mood. 'I realised it tonight when I was talking to the Superintendent.'

He sighed. 'I was pretty clear about myself Thursday, when we were in the car,' he admitted gloomily. 'However mad it seemed at the time, we ought to have just kept on driving. I haven't been very intelligent.'

I stepped back from him and walked down the room because I could not bear to be close to him any longer, and as soon as he was out of reach I felt I could not bear that either. I sat down at the table and he stood looking at me wistfully.

'What are you thinking?' he enquired at last.

I opened my mouth to reply, changed my mind and shrugged my shoulders. I could not bring myself to say it, but there was a dead body between us. We'd got to find out about Victor. He was watching me closely, and presently he grinned at me wryly with rather heartbreaking fondness.

'You're not so much conventional as civilised, aren't you, Liz?' he said, and settled himself on the arm of the chair by the fireplace.

I put my elbows on the table and rested my head in my hands while the nightmare settled over me again.

'I didn't know those blue flowers meant "success," did you?' I demanded inconsequentially.

'No, and I'm not at all sure of it now,' he observed promptly. 'I challenged that when they produced it. It was only some tale of a char's. The copper didn't seem too sold on it himself. That was one of the things which made me feel that they had very little evidence against anybody. A perfectly idiotic story.' He glanced at me with abrupt directness. 'They told me you had done the shooting.'

'Did you believe it?'

He appeared utterly scandalised. That was the best thing about Andy, he was the sanest thing on earth.

'Hardly,' he said stiffly. 'I assured them they could cross that idea off their list to start with. I said that the last time I'd seen you you were determined to keep your marriage going if it suffocated you. That's what made me so depressed.'

'Did you say that in so many words?'

He nodded and grimaced at me. 'That wasn't very clever. After that they started worrying about my movements. I'd met Victor Lane at the club bar.'

'But only for five minutes,' I put in hastily.

He slid down into the chair and leaned back, his hands behind his wiry black head.

'Long enough to take a dislike to him,' he said distinctly. 'I was prejudiced, no doubt, but I did hate his guts. He wasn't our sort at all, Liz. That sort of sneery smart conceit always means a shallow chap. Oh well, that's over. Anyway, after I'd met him and loathed him I didn't feel like being sociable, so I went off for a walk. I got into a lane I found beside the course and after a while I sat down on the bank and tried to sort out what I'd better do. It was obvious that I couldn't avoid you if I stayed in the town, but on the other hand I thought it might prejudice me with the profession if I threw up the job and cleared out. I thought I might get a reputation for instability at the outset of my career. So all that had to be weighed up. There was quite a lot to be considered one way and another, and it took me the whole afternoon before I came to a decision.'

I watched him helplessly. 'You thought you'd go.'

'Yes,' he agreed briskly, 'yes. It seemed the lesser of two evils. I knew I'd make love to you if ever I saw you again so I walked back to the club, picked up the car and drove into town to fix up about leaving. Not much of an alibi, as it happens, because I've got no witnesses and I seem to have been only a quarter of a mile from the cottage all the time.'

'Did you hear the shot?'

He frowned. 'They asked me that. The trouble is I don't know. I was so preoccupied. As I was walking along just before I sat down I did think I heard something in the distance, but I'd only left the clubhouse then and Lane went off only a few minutes before I did. If that *was* the shot, he must have been potted almost as soon as he stepped in the cottage, which doesn't seem feasible.'

I sat staring at him in undisguised dismay. 'Didn't you see anybody at all? Didn't anyone pass you?' As an alibi it was worse than mine.

'No one of any use,' he said. 'One car went by, but it was blinding. I don't think the driver could have noticed me. I fancy it was a Morris Eight, but I didn't notice the colour or the number. They're going to broadcast for the driver, but I can't imagine there's any hope of him turning up or being any use if he does. The only other living soul who passed down the road when I was there is now in hospital, unconscious, and is not expected to recover. He's one of the masters here, by the way.'

'Mr. Rorke?'

'That's the man.' He seemed surprised. 'You've heard about him, have you? He came down the lane while I was sitting there and he eyed me, but we didn't speak. I'd never seen him before and he was in a fine old state. I thought he was a tramp. When I described him the police recognised him at once. He'd been to the club and they'd slung him out.'

'I saw him start from the school,' I remarked. 'He'd been trying to sober up under a shower, that's why he was so wet. What was he doing in the lane?'

Andy shrugged his shoulders. 'The police say he was taking a short cut to the London Road. A truck driver has reported giving him a lift as far as the northern suburbs. After that the poor beast seems to have had an argument with a double-decker bus, so he won't be able to help much. Not that it matters.'

I sat up at that. 'But it does matter,' I objected. 'I don't think you understand. Uncle Fred South—'

'Who's that? Old turnip-face, the Superintendent?'

'Call him what you like,' I insisted, 'but he's no fool. You imagine he's let you out to come up here because he hadn't any evidence to hold you. Well, my bet is that he did it on purpose. He's slippery, he's—'

'My dear girl, he wasn't there,' he interjected. 'For the final three hours or so I was interviewed by a mere Inspector and a brace of helmetless bobbies. The Inspector read a report which came in to him and let it out quite casually that you were up here alone. When I insisted that in that case I was coming up myself he tried to object. I called his bluff by pointing out that he must charge me if he was going to hold me, and after a bit he gave way. I wasn't followed here, Liz. The road was perfectly clear.'

I was not satisfied. 'It's the gun,' I said, 'that's what they're worrying about. It's because they can't connect you with Victor's gun that they haven't arrested you. They think I must have given it to you somehow.'

He thought that one over and I saw I'd got the point home.

'I knew where it was kept, you see,' I added. 'They found my fingerprints on the drawer, I expect.'

'But that's ridiculous,' he protested. 'What does that prove? I knew where the gun was kept for that matter.'

'*You* did?'

'Of course I did. In the top middle drawer of his desk. Everybody knew it. It was one of the first things I ever heard about Victor Lane when I first came to the town. "A colourful personality," so I was told. "Kept a loaded revolver in the top middle drawer of his desk. So dashing and original." I thought it sounded dangerous. Well, it's proved so, hasn't it?'

'But, Andy,' I exclaimed, horror-stricken, 'you didn't tell the police this, did you?'

'No,' he admitted seriously. 'Being cautious by nature, I forbore. But I assure you it was common knowledge. Provincial people like whispering things like that. It makes home sound like the movies. When did you look in the drawer? Yesterday?'

'Yes,' I said slowly, trying to remember about a thing which was as remote as if it had happened ten years before. 'I went into the study once the day before, when I first got in from the ride with you, but I didn't go up to the desk. I was looking for Victor, but the only person there was Bickky Seckker.'

'Who's that?'

I told him and he listened with interest. 'What was he doing there alone?'

'He wasn't near the desk,' I assured him, smiling at the idea of the gentle Mr. Seckker being in any way concerned with the theft of a revolver. 'He was at the fireplace on the other side of the room, burning something, I think.'

Andy was puzzled. 'Destroying the documents, as in a spy play?' he enquired politely.

'No, only burning a sheet of paper. I think he said he'd been trying to light his pipe with it.'

'Extraordinary.' Andy spoke without excitement. 'An odd place, though. No place for you and me, Liz. To fit in with Tinworth we'd have to have been born here. We'll have to get out of it, and out of the country, just as soon as we can. I love you. I love you, darling, more than anything in the world.'

I leant across the table, my hand outstretched. 'It's good to hear you say it, my dear.'

As Andy stumbled to his feet to come

towards me the door behind me opened. I felt the draught on my neck and turned just in time to see a familiar clown's face looming in out of the shadow of the staircase. Uncle Fred South stepped lightly into the room and closed the door behind him.

'Perhaps I ought to have knocked,' he said, and his country voice was broader and slyer than ever.

Andy turned on him savagely, his face dark with blood and his eyes furious.

'Do you always walk into people's houses unannounced, Superintendent? The ordinary laws of the country don't affect the police down here, I suppose?'

Uncle was unabashed. 'I haven't walked in because I ain't been out, Doctor,' he said pleasantly, favouring me with an alarming battery of confidential twinkles. 'I changed my mind. I thought I wouldn't leave Mrs. Lane in this great set of buildings all alone, so I went to the study, which we've made our headquarters, and sat there writing my report. Then, I don't know how it was, I must have fallen asleep in the chair.' He smiled at me, his face glowing with good temper. 'I reckon it was that pudding that did it,' he said.

He did not expect to be believed but it was impossible to be angry with him. He was so cheerful about it all.

'I came up for some of my equipment,' he went on placidly. 'I always carry it about with me because I don't like to see a constable scribbling in the corner whilst I'm conducting an interview. It doesn't seem friendly. This equipment is not official. I bought it meself. Out of the proceeds of the last Police Concert, as a matter of fact. I left it up here by mistake.'

Andy and I stood staring at him, mystified but with growing apprehension. As we watched he dived under the white-draped table and came up with a box which looked like a portable radio set. A flex which had been attached to the candle lamp which we used at the evening meal hung limply from its side. The Superintendent put it gently on the table.

'Well I never did!' he said calmly. 'My little old tape recorder's been on all the time.'

There was a long and dreadful pause. We all three stood looking at the little machine, its turntables moving silently on the open top.

Andy sprang towards it and just as quickly a broad body inserted itself between him and the moving tape.

'Wait a minute, son,' said Uncle Fred South. He edged himself round until he stood facing us, but still shielding the wicked little machine. 'Now look here, you two,' he began, his round-eyed glance flickering from one to the other of us in shrewd appraisal, 'I'm more than twice as old as either of you and that gives me a right to speak, policeman or not. What I want to tell you is this. I'm not against you and I'm not for

163

you. In this business I've got just about as much heart as this table I'm sitting on, but I'm just as sound as it and just as useful as it too.' He was speaking with tremendous sincerity and managed to be strangely impressive. I know we both stepped back. 'If you've killed a man between you I'll turn you in,' he went on. 'I shan't hang you, because that ain't my business, but I'll hand you over to the law and the lawyers and I'll read about you in the papers and never give you another thought. But if you're innocent I'll get you out of this here business so fast you won't know you've ever been in it, and we shan't have a pack of London legal-eagles upsetting all our summer holidays and keeping us all standing about until Christmas.'

He paused and, after giving me a steady, not unfriendly stare, concentrated on Andy, whose dark face was unrevealing.

'Now, I told this young woman in this very room not so long ago that if I once knew the footing you two were on I'd tell you things about yourselves you didn't even know,' he announced. 'That is why I fitted up this here little arrangement and set it going as soon as I heard your car come up the Tortham Road. I'd sent word to my Inspector to let you go, and I figured out that you'd come straight up here if you heard that Mrs. Lane had been left in the school alone. There's nothing against you in that. In your position I'd have done the same.

164

Now I could have had a fellow listening and taking everything down in shorthand, and that would have been in order. But I didn't do that because there's a great deal of difference between the spoken word and what's been taken down by a chap with a pencil, and I didn't just want to catch you out. I wanted the truth, and by gee I'm going to get it. Will you sit quiet while I play this through to the three of us? That's the honest way. If there's a bit I don't understand, then we'll take it back and listen again.'

There was silence for a while. My mouth was dry and I felt sick with fear, not because I was guilty but because I couldn't remember anything we'd said and because he was going to find out that Andy and I were in love after all. I glanced at Andy, but he was watching the Superintendent, an odd, defiant expression on his face. Without looking at me he thrust an arm round my shoulders so that we stood together.

'All right,' he said.

The old man sighed. 'That's more like it,' he said. 'Sit down. It'll make you shy, you know. Still, we can't help that. Now listen.'

The dreadful performance began. I had not dreamed that ordinary conversation went so slowly. It was terrible. Every word seemed to have twice its normal meaning, and the pauses to go on forever. Andy's voice I knew. It sounded exactly as it always did, very much alive and deeper in tone than most men's. But who the breathy young woman with the squeak in her voice was I could not believe until I heard her saying the things I'd said. Andy and I sat side by side at the table and stared down at our hands clenched on the cloth. But Uncle Fred South just watched the machine, his eyes half closed and his shining knobbly face quite expressionless.

It went on and on. The whole picture was there but it was magnified. We sounded as if we were overacting, and when I heard Andy admitting once again that he had known where Victor kept his gun my heart turned slowly over and I could scarcely breathe. I stole a glance at the Superintendent after that, but he had not moved.

Yet the really damaging passage took me by surprise. It seemed to spring out of its context and to obliterate every other line. It was Andy's voice, calm and matter-of-fact yet full of determination.

'We'll have to get out of it, and out of the country, just as soon as we can. I love you, darling, more than anything in the world.'

I did not hear my reply. I was looking hopelessly at Uncle Fred South and he was sitting up, a wide broad smile which yet had something grim in it spreading over his face. The recording went on; the Superintendent's own voice and the sound of Andy's protest as he heard it were all faithfully reproduced. We did not move.

At last the Superintendent leaned forward and switched off the recorder and there was a long silence.

I spoke first. I could not bear the suspense any longer, and the grim smile on the shrewd yet comical face of the old man seemed to fill the world.

'Well?' I said huskily. 'Now you know the—the footing we're on, what can you tell us about ourselves that we don't know?'

He rose to his feet and sniffed. Something had happened to him. His whole attitude towards us had changed. He looked tired and somehow more ordinary and when his eyes met mine there was no knowing twinkle in them. Andy sat stiffly at the table, his dark face sullen and quiet.

'Have you found out anything you did not know, Superintendent?'

Uncle Fred South cocked an eye at him. 'Yes,' he said distinctly, 'I've got my man, and I'd have had him before and we'd all have had a night's rest if this young woman had thought to open her mouth earlier.'

I stared. The ground was opening beneath my feet.

'It's not true—' I was beginning when he turned on me.

'Now pay attention,' he said. 'The police don't give witnesses explanations. Silent and mysterious, that's the line the police take in an

167

enquiry, and then it's all a nice surprise for everybody when the evidence comes out in court. But because you've been very helpful, and because it won't make a mite of difference anyway in this particular case, I'll tell you. I'll be as good as my word. I'll tell you something you didn't know about yourselves. You didn't know you could tell me who killed Victor Lane. Does that surprise you?'

I put my hand in Andy's and looked at the Superintendent.

'How did I tell you?'

He shook his head at me wearily. 'You told your young man, you didn't tell me,' he said calmly. 'You told me who burned the sheet of paper in the fireplace in the study. That was the important thing.'

My universe performed a dizzy somersault.

'Mr. Seckker!' I exclaimed incredulously. 'I don't believe it.'

'I don't ask you to.' He sat down again and leant across the table. 'I could lose my pension gossiping like this,' he murmured, lowering his voice to elude, no doubt, the long ears of Tinworth strained to hear. 'That bit of paper was the first thing we found. It was charred but intact and we got a nice pic from it very quickly. It turned out to be a little document that this whole town has heard about, on and off, for the past year or more. It was the Pitcher boy's examination paper.'

We looked at him blankly and he laughed.

'You two seem to be the only people in this place who don't know what goes on,' he said. 'You're "foreigners," that's your trouble. The Pitcher boy is a nice little boy who comes from a very strait-laced home. He had the misfortune to turn in a very silly bit of work for his end-of-term exam last winter and—'

'Oh!' I exclaimed as Mrs. Veal's story came back to me. 'And Mr. Rorke wrote something on it.'

'That's it, that's it.' The knowing gleam had returned to the round eyes and Uncle Fred South was himself again, encouraging me as a promising pupil. 'Mr. Rorke was a bit elated, shall we say, at the time when he corrected it and he wrote a few terse Anglo-Saxon words at the bottom of the sheet and sent it back to the boy. The boy sent it to his pa, who had no more sense than to send it to the Headmaster, and the Headmaster . . .' He broke off and his twinkle vanished and he looked at me with unusual kindliness. 'Mr. Lane's dead, isn't he, poor fellow?' he said. 'So we mustn't judge him. But he could be hard, and, saving your presence, Mrs Lane, he could be dirty in business and no mistake. He held that bit of paper over the man Rorke. He'd only got to show it, you see, and the man would never get another job in a good school.'

Andy drew a long breath. He looked utterly astounded.

'But did everybody know this?' he

demanded.

'Oh yes, Doctor.' Uncle Fred South appeared equally surprised that anyone should query that point. 'Rorke made no secret of it to his few friends, and in Tinworth if you've told one you've told all. Lane said he'd destroy the paper if Rorke went on the water wagon. Rorke did. It must have cost him something, but he had strength, that man. Then at the end of this term he went to Mr. Lane and asked him for his release and a reference and for the paper to be destroyed. Lane refused but said he'd think it over. That was on the Wednesday. Rorke came down the town and told one or two people about it. I'd heard it myself before the night was out.' He cleared his throat and leaned back in his chair. 'We don't have a lot to talk about, Doctor, so we talk about each other. That's human nature.'

'But'—Andy thrust his long hands through his wiry black hair—'if you knew all this why didn't you suspect Rorke in the first place?'

'We did. I made sure of it.' The Superintendent's eyes were round as shillings. 'Naturally, as soon as I heard that Rorke was the last person to see Lane alive I made sure of it. But as soon as I got into the study, what did I find? Why, the document destroyed. If the body had been there beside it, well, it would have been simple. But it wasn't there. Lane was known to have been at the golf club for lunch. When he left Rorke he was alive.

We worked it out that he'd destroyed the document in front of Rorke when they were both there together, so we didn't expect the young man to go after him and kill him once he'd got what he wanted. It wouldn't have been reasonable, would it?'

He was silent for a moment. 'Now, of course, I can see it all,' he went on. 'Lane refused Rorke and went off to the golf course. Rorke took the Headmaster's gun and followed him.' He nodded at Andy. 'You were quite right when you said someone must have waited for Mr. Lane in the cottage and shot him as soon as he appeared. That's what Rorke did. Then he hitchhiked to London and—well, poor fellow, it's saved us a lot of trouble. He can't last. His back's broken.'

'Bickky Seckker,' I began slowly and the Superintendent caught me up.

'Bickky Seckker hasn't been questioned. No one saw any point in asking *him* anything. But I bet I know what *he* did. I've known him for years. It's just what he would do. I bet he was up in his classroom waiting to see what happened at Rorke's interview with Lane. I'll be bound he saw the Headmaster drive off and Rorke come reeling out just after him, and I bet he went down to the study to see if things had been settled. He found the exam paper hadn't been destroyed, and it so shocked him that he took matters into his own hands, burned it there and then, and was caught redhanded when Mrs. Lane appeared. That's about it.'

'But how would he know where it was?' I demanded, fascinated by this pyrotechnic display in the art of deduction. 'If Rorke didn't, how would Bickky?'

Uncle Fred South laughed outright. 'Bickky has been in this school for more years than I've been in Tinworth,' he said. 'Depend upon it, there ain't much he doesn't know.'

He moved towards the door, a plump and even joyous figure on his light feet.

'Doctor,' he said, holding out his hand to Andy, 'you made a very intelligent remark on that there machine of mine. You said that you young people ought to get out of Tinworth right away, and afterwards out of the country. Good luck to you. But later on, in a year or so or maybe more, come back and see us all.' He grinned. 'You'll find you'll know a lot more about us then, and we're remarkably nice people once you get to know us. A little bit inquisitive perhaps, but, think of the time it saves. Good night to you both. If there's anything I can ever do for you, you know where to find me.'

When the door had closed behind him, Andy turned to me.